COLDER THAN THE GRAVE

Green eyes, hair like a burning sunset: the men couldn't take their eyes off the widow at the funeral. When she told private eye Paul Lomax what her problem was, he thought she'd gone grief-crazy. He figured the case would be more hassle than a roundup on a kangaroo farm, but he needed the cash and she seemed to have stacks. And when he began his investigation into the drugs scene and the beautiful women who were its victims, all hell broke loose . . .

D0264612

RAYMOND HAIGH

COLDER THAN THE GRAVE

Complete and Unabridged

LINFORD
Leicester

First published in Great Britain in 1984 by
Robert Hale Limited
London

First Linford Edition
published 2003
by arrangement with
Robert Hale Limited
London

British Library CIP Data

Haigh, Raymond
    Colder than the grave.—Large print ed.—
Linford mystery library
    1. Detective and mystery stories
    2. Large type books
    I. Title
    823.9'14 [F]

ISBN 0–7089–4967–3

Published by
F. A. Thorpe (Publishing)
Anstey, Leicestershire

Set by Words & Graphics Ltd.
Anstey, Leicestershire
Printed and bound in Great Britain by
T. J. International Ltd., Padstow, Cornwall

This book is printed on acid-free paper

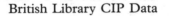

1

I looked at her across the open grave. She stood perfectly erect, the padded shoulders of her exclusive black suit somehow emphasising her upright posture. Her eyes were indistinct behind a black-spotted veil that flared out from her cute little pill-box hat. Black gloved hands clasped a tiny black handbag, slender legs were sheathed in black silk stockings. Detached, aloof from it all, she seemed to be dissociating herself from the proceedings, putting herself a million miles away from what was going on around her.

'O God, receive the soul of Thy servant Carl. Appoint holy angels to lead him into Paradise. Release him from . . . '

The white haired old priest intoned the litany, straps tightened under the coffin, the pallbearers began to lower it into the grave. I caught the odour of freshly dug earth and with it the sickly sweet smell of flowers wilting in the hot, August sun.

'Eternal rest give unto him, O lord . . . '
The priest dipped a silver handled brush into a bowl of holy water and sprinkled the coffin in a final blessing. ' . . . And let perpetual light shine upon him.'

He replenished the brush and offered it to the widow. She ignored the gesture: just stood there, erect and cold as the earth in the grave.

Still murmuring prayers, the priest handed the brush to the man beside her who dutifully sent a rain of drops splashing down onto the polished wood. He passed it along, and one by one the mourners around the rim of the grave gave the body a watery benediction.

'May he rest in peace. Amen.' The priest closed the prayer book, drew a ribbon of purple silk from about his neck, kissed it, and wrapped it around his hand. He took the widow gently by the arm, turned her away from the grave, and started back to the road. She kept her high-heels rock steady as she led the mourners across sheets of plastic grass that covered the disturbed earth. Some angel of a seamstress had toiled over her suit. The fit was a shade too perfect for the occasion, and silky material was revealing every movement of her slender body.

We trod our way between the graves to the cars lined up on the narrow strip of tarmac. I watched the old priest shake her hand, then some funeral director's flunkey opened the door of a black limousine and every male eye lingered on her elegant legs as they were drawn up into the car. I slid behind the wheel of my dark-green three-and-a-half-litre Rover, started the engine, then followed the cortege out onto the main Barfield Road.

I saw Estelle Bergman for the first time there at the graveside. Seeing her had only made me more curious to know why she needed a private investigator so desperately.

2

By one-thirty the few remaining mourners were leaving the big Victorian house that sat on the crest of Mount St. Joseph, a suburb of Barfield that still has a lot of class. Through the bay window at the front of the high room I could see clear over the rooftops to the moors that nudge the western edges of the town.

I caught the murmuring of condolences, the sound of farewells, the slamming of a heavy door. Then Estelle Bergman came back into the room and walked towards me. I rose to my feet and took the hand she offered. It was small and soft and remained limp in mine while I did the shaking.

'I'm sorry to have kept you here so long, Mr Lomax, but I couldn't explain things to you until we were alone.' Her voice was whispery, almost childlike: it made me think of fragile china and rustling leaves. Refined and unaffected, there was no accent to betray her origins.

'Won't you sit down again. And perhaps you'll let me get you something to drink while I explain.'

I eased myself back into the leather chesterfield. 'I'd appreciate a whisky.'

Her generous mouth relaxed into a tired smile. 'Of course,' she said. She crossed over to a collection of bottles and decanters that were arranged on top of a long, rosewood sideboard. 'Anything with it?'

'Do you have any ice?' Strong afternoon sunlight was flooding the room and making it uncomfortably warm.

She opened one of the rosewood doors and I could see the illuminated interior of a small refrigerator. Ice rattled into glasses, I heard the soft thud of the refrigerator door closing. She came back, handed me a tall glass half filled with ice and spirit, then gently lowered herself into the chesterfield facing mine.

I gazed at her across a couple of yards of Persian carpet. She wasn't wearing the hat with the cute little veil now. I could see her features clearly: big green eyes that were bright beneath delicately shaded lids, small straight nose, generous mouth, firm chin. Her complexion was pale. I guessed it wasn't the shock of sudden bereavement that had made it that way. It probably always was. Smooth, pale skin always seems to team up with hair that's like a burning sunset.

She pressed the cold glass against her cheek and closed her eyes. Her body became limp with a sudden surrender to weariness. 'Dear God,' she moaned tearfully, 'I'm so confused. I just don't know how to begin.'

'Why not begin by telling me how your husband died, Mrs Bergman,' I said gently. 'I'm sure that will bring us round to talking about how I can help you.'

The green eyes snapped open, her body tensed. In a voice that held more conviction than a martyr's prayer she said, 'I'm afraid I can't tell you how my husband died, Mr Lomax, because he's not dead.'

I was looking at her warily now. My own experience told me that the shock and grief of sudden bereavement can make people disturbed for a while. Maybe this was her way of coping with the tragedy: just denying it had ever happened.

'You husband isn't dead?'

She laughed. It was a bitter, tearful sound. 'You don't believe me, do you? The police refused to, so I suppose it was too much to expect that you would.'

'But the burial, this afternoon?'

'That wasn't my husband. I've no idea whose body was in the coffin.'

I decided I'd better go along with her for a while. 'What makes you so sure, Mrs Bergman? How do you know it wasn't your husband?'

'I suppose the best thing I can do is start at the beginning,' she said. 'Ten days ago, when the police called: a sergeant and a police woman. They tried to break it to me gently. They told me that Carl had been in an accident: a fatal accident.'

She took a sip from her glass. Her hair had been arranged on top of her head so she could wear the hat. She reached up; slender fingers with vermilion nails plucked out a comb and some pins. She shook her head and waves of copper-gold cascaded down onto her shoulders. She seemed more comfortable with her hair down. Another sip at her drink and she was ready to go on.

'They said someone had to try and identify the body. The car had been on fire and the man inside was badly burnt. They made it clear I didn't have to do it: a relative or close friend would have been all right. I suppose they were being kind really. Trying to spare me the shock of seeing . . . seeing . . . Oh, God, I never realised a human body could be so appallingly disfigured.'

She shuddered. Her glossy red lips started to tremble. She swallowed some more of her drink, coughed as it went down, then said: 'There was no one near who could do it. No friends, no relatives. Anyway, I wanted to identify the body. I'd have felt I was letting Carl down if I'd not. They took me to Barfield General Hospital: it was in the mortuary, in a metal drawer. They wouldn't let me see the face and head. They said the damage was so bad there wouldn't be any point. They kept it covered with a white cloth. The policewoman put her arms around me and then they pulled the sheet from the body. It was indescribable. Most of the flesh was wrinkled and black. There were cavities where the skin had charred through. And the smell . . . like . . . like burning meat.'

She screwed her eyes tight shut, as if to dispel the vision she'd summoned up for me. Presently she said, 'Only a small part of the body hadn't been burnt. There was a swathe of white skin across the chest. They told me later he'd been lying on his arm and the flames hadn't had time to penetrate.' Her voice petered out. She was breathing heavily, maybe trying to control a feeling of nausea. The light dusting of powder on her face couldn't hide the film of sweat that was beginning to gleam on her brow.

'Do you want to stop there for a while?' I said softly.

She opened her eyes again. 'No. I've got to get it over with now.' She drained her glass and went on: 'A kind of nightmare panic had been building up inside me from the minute the police brought me the news. Standing there, in the mortuary, with the fire blackened body, the stench of formalin and burnt flesh, the cloth covered head, that snake of hairy white skin . . . I just screamed. One, long, drawn out scream. And when my breath was gone everything went black. I came-to in a private room in the hospital. The policewoman was still there. They treated me for shock; kept me in until the next day because there was no one for them to contact. A couple of days later they came and took me to the police station to identify the belongings they'd salvaged from the car. The remains of a wristwatch, a ring, a document case that had been locked in the boot, some coins and a bunch of keys.'

'Were they your husband's things?'

'The ring was, and the document case had his name in tiny letters on the side. I recognised the bunch of keys, but the watch could have been anybody's: you could hardly tell it was a watch.'

I sensed she'd recounted the worst part. Her breathing was gentler now, and she seemed more composed. She leant forward and put her glass on a pile of high-class fashion magazines that were stacked on a coffee table.

'The inquest was held a few days ago,' she went on. 'The police and the coroner were very considerate. It must have seemed an open and shut case to them. Everyone just assumed that it was Carl who had died in the car. I did too, at first, but I just couldn't get that snake of unburnt skin out of my mind. You see, Mr Lomax, they'd got me pretty heavily sedated, and what with that and the trauma of it all I couldn't think clearly. It wasn't until after the inquest that I realised what my subconscious had been trying to tell me: that some marks were missing from that patch of skin.' Her weak little voice petered out again.

'You mean some scar or birthmark. A tattoo, perhaps?' I prompted.

'Not exactly, Mr Lomax. But it was

a distinct mark that would have clearly identified my husband. And it wasn't there.'

I looked puzzled. 'Could you be a little more specific, Mrs Bergman?'

'You're married, aren't you, Mr Lomax?' she countered. 'You certainly look as if you are.' Two patches of colour appeared on her cheeks and began to spread.

'I was once, a long time ago.'

'Surely not so long ago you've forgotten the kind of things that happen between married people, or lovers perhaps.'

I didn't say a word. Just raised an eyebrow and went on looking at her.

Her mouth pulled into an embarrassed little smile. 'Really, Mr Lomax, do I have to spell it out for you. I bit him: on a certain part of his chest. It was a hard bite that drew blood and left a ring of teeth marks. I did it the morning of the accident, but there was no mark of that kind on the body in the mortuary.'

'Why didn't you tell the police all this?'

'I did. The day before the funeral. Like I told you, before that I'd been so shocked and confused I hadn't realised the marks were missing.'

'And what did they say?'

She began to colour up again when she recalled the encounter. 'The chief inspector was very patient with me, but I could tell he thought I was just some hysterical woman who couldn't come to terms with her husband's death. He told me all the legal procedures had been carefully observed and advised me to have a word with my doctor.'

'But you were still convinced the missing marks meant that the body in the car couldn't be your husband's?'

She shook her head. 'I wish I had been that certain, Mr Lomax, but I'd be lying to you if I said I was. It was something that happened early this morning that convinced me that Carl is still alive. The dawn chorus woke me. I couldn't get back to sleep so I came down to the kitchen and made some tea.' She inclined her head towards the far end of the room. 'I was standing by that window and I saw a man watching the house from beneath the trees at the bottom of the garden. He looked up at

13

me for a few seconds, then he turned and headed off down the slope.'

'Did you recognise this man?'

'I could hardly fail to, Mr Lomax. It was my husband.'

3

I relaxed back in the chesterfield and gazed across at her. It was much more than pleasant. I got to thinking she could bite me whenever she wanted. I could stand the pain if she could stand the taste. I made a supreme effort and dragged my thoughts back to the business in hand.

'Surely, Mrs Bergman, the police checked the body against your husband's dental records?'

She gave a resigned sigh. 'You still don't believe me, do you? We've only been in England for a year. We were married less than three years ago. For all I know my husband has never visited a dentist. He's not even bothered to register with a doctor over here.'

'What were the coroner's findings?'

'Accidental death. It could hardly have been anything else. The car crashed into the arch of an old railway bridge on a minor road not far from here.'

'What time was the accident?' I asked.

'The landlady of a pub not far from the bridge called the police about one-thirty in the morning. She said she'd seen the flames through her bedroom window.'

'It wouldn't be unusual for him to be heading home at that time, then?'

'My husband's a freelance journalist. He has to take commissions when they come, follow up stories as they develop. His work takes him away from home quite a bit. Even when he is at home it's not unusual for him to be out at that time, even later. But you must get one thing absolutely clear, Mr Lomax: it wasn't my husband in that car.'

'If it wasn't him why hasn't he contacted you? Where do you think he is? And why should he be watching the house just after dawn?'

'Don't you think I've been asking myself all those questions?' she retorted. 'He's in some kind of trouble. I know he is.'

She rose to her feet. It was one, continuous feline movement. She strode over to a massive Victorian fireplace. Two pubescent marble wood-nymphs were holding up a mantel that would have crushed a dozen navvies.

She turned and faced me, then said, 'He's been working on something special for the past nine months. He's putting together a series of articles on the drugs scene. You know, investigative journalism, that sort of thing. One of the Sunday papers has made him a big advance on it. I sometimes think it's become an obsession with him.'

She spoke of her husband in the present tense. Her conviction that he was alive seemed unshakeable. She looked tired, and fear was shining out of those big green eyes: a fear that was tangible enough to stop a ten-ton truck.

'I've got a feeling this drug thing's at the heart of it all,' she said in a whispery, tearful voice. 'I think he's found out too much. Uncovered something very nasty. I think he's hiding somewhere because he daren't come to this house. Maybe it's being watched. Sometimes, Mr Lomax, I almost hate the way he earns his money.'

She moved back to where I was sitting

and looked down at me. In the sultry heat of that August afternoon her perfume seemed to envelop her in coolness. Up close, the sweet fragrance dispelled the odours of carpets and polish and leather that were heavy in the room. A barely perceptible trembling seemed to have touched her lips and spread throughout her body. Presently she said, 'Will you help me, Mr Lomax? Help me find my husband and extricate him from whatever trouble he's in.'

I eyed her steadily. If she was right about her husband the job could be more hassle than a round-up on a kangaroo farm. If she wasn't, then I'd almost be stealing her money. I had no other client on the books at that time, but a dozen creditors had me on theirs. Solvency demanded I took the case, but to ease my conscience I began to warn her about the cost, started giving her details of my daily charges.

She raised a hand. 'Money isn't a problem, Mr Lomax. My husband's been doing very well since we came to England. And anyway, I've money of my own.'

I didn't respond. I just went on looking up into that pale, almost too perfect face.

After a few seconds more of the silence she repeated, 'Will you help me, Mr Lomax?' Her weak little voice was low and her eyes were begging me.

I nodded. 'Sure I'll help you, Mrs Bergman.'

Her body relaxed when I said that. The trembling stopped and relief washed over her face. 'Thank you, Mr Lomax. You'll never know how grateful I am. I think I'd better show you up to my husband's study and let you take a look around.'

She led me out of the room and into the hallway. The layers of old paint had been stripped from the deep skirtings and panelled doors, and the pine had been varnished to give it a dull sheen. The walls were lined out with coffee-coloured hessian, and there were plenty of modern lithographs and engravings in aluminium frames. The size of the place, the high white ceiling with its deep cornices, the chic decor, made it seem like a quiet backwater in some city art gallery.

We headed across oatmeal-coloured

carpet, passed through an archway and began to climb a massive flight of stairs. Someone had been busy with paint stripper on the handrail and balusters; the varnished pine was gleaming in the golden, afternoon sunlight.

I followed close behind her, enjoying the liquid movement of the rise and fall of her hips. She pulled ahead as we rounded the landing, and I began to take in the swaying hem of her skirt, slender ankles under black silk stockings, black high-heeled shoes.

We went into a smallish room at the back of the house: what might once have been a child's or a maid's bedroom. It was an office now. A battered Olivetti portable typewriter was resting in the middle of a neat and orderly desk. There was a blue extension phone beside it. A china mug, decorated with clowns, was crammed with pens and pencils. Beneath the window, a small glass-fronted book-case held a pharmacopoeia, Shaw's Pharmaceutical Chemistry, a medical dictionary and some text books.

She picked up an envelope from the

desk, shook out a photograph and handed it to me. Clear and sharp, it had been cut from a larger print to leave only the head and shoulders of a man wearing a tuxedo. Plenty of dark curly hair, calculating blue eyes, a wide sensual mouth that wasn't smiling. I guessed he'd be a few years older than his wife, probably around thirty-five.

'How old is your husband?' I asked. 'And how tall?'

'He'll be thirty-one next month. He's about five feet eleven, not as tall as you. Deep tan, athletic muscular build.'

She gestured towards a nest of metal drawers. 'Some of the material he's gathered for the article on the drugs scene is in there.'

I slid out one of the shallow drawers to reveal an assortment of some drug company's handouts, the kind of soft-sell advertising material they mail to doctors. I pushed it back and opened the one below. It held a card index system that seemed to contain details of articles and books on drugs.

'Working on an assignment like that he

must have had contacts, people he needed to interview. Where would he keep names and addresses?'

'He didn't keep anything like that in here,' she said. 'I suppose it would have been too sensitive. He had a notebook that he always carried around with him. I would imagine names, addresses, things like that, are all in there. He was very careful with it.'

'Do you have the document case the police salvaged from the car?'

She nodded, 'Wait here a moment and I'll get it.'

She stepped out of the office, crossed the landing and went into a pink carpeted bedroom. Through the open doors I could see a double bed with a headboard of quilted pink silk. A smooth coverlet of matching silk was stretched over the bed. There was a range of ivory and gold fitted wardrobes and a built-in dressing table against the far wall. Not the usual department store stuff: these were decorated with some deep carvings, French Empire style. It was a strangely opulent contrast to the stark modern treatment of the ground floor rooms. She reached down beside the bed, picked up a case and came back into the office.

I took it from her and rested it on the edge of the desk. It was the kind of thing a smart, up-and-coming young executive would pack his low-calorie lunch in. Black leather with the handle and catches recessed into a polished aluminium frame. The owner's name was spelt out on the leather in tiny silver letters. It had seen a lot of use: the frame was scratched and dinted and the leather was scuffed. I slid the catches back and the lid clicked open. There was an assortment of pens and pencils, a folded newspaper, a couple of shorthand notebooks, one of those microscopic tape recorders that are used for dictating letters, some more of the soft-sell drug pamphlets and a clear polythene bag that had been sealed with staples driven through a coroner's-office tag.

I flicked through the shorthand note-books. The pages were blank but some thin strips of paper left in the spiral bindings said leaves had been torn out.

'Not all of those things were in the case,' she said. I cleared out the pockets of Carl's suits and put the things I found in there. Nothing much though, just the newspaper and a few pens.'

I glanced at the newspaper. It was an evening edition of the Barfield Echo, dated almost a month earlier.

'Have you tried the tape recorder?' I asked.

She nodded. 'I ran the spool through both ways as soon as the police returned the document case. It's completely blank.'

I picked up the sealed polythene bag. 'May I?'

'Why not?'

I tore it open and shook the contents onto the lid of the case. Some coins, the remains of a watch and a bunch of keys. 'Do you recognise any of these?' I passed the keys to her.

Vermilion nails eased them round the ring as she murmured, 'Garage, front door, back door, desk, car, document case . . . ' She faltered, 'I don't know what these are for.' She held up a latch key and a small mortice lock key, then laid the bunch on the palm of my hand. The metal had been discoloured by heat. Presumably they'd been in the ignition lock whilst the car was burning.

'Could we take a look at the spot where you saw your husband yesterday? I'll have to sift through these papers, but perhaps I could come back tomorrow and spend the morning here.'

I returned the fire-damaged items to the polythene bag, then placed it, along with the cut-down photograph, in the document case and snapped it shut.

'May I take this?' I asked.

'I don't see why not, Mr Lomax, but take good care of it. My husband's going to want it back.' I heard the tremor in her voice and wondered whose morale she was trying to boost: hers or mine.

We went back to the ground floor. She took me into a big kitchen. Plenty of solid mahogany cupboards, split-level cooker, double-bowl sink unit, walk-in size fridge and a lot of fancy Italian wall tiling. I figured investigative journalism might be risky but it seemed to have its rewards. Or maybe she'd splashed out with some of the money she'd said was her own.

She opened a door located beneath the head of the stairs and we went down stone steps. The brick walls were painted white and the air felt damp and cool. Through open doorways I could make out a boiler room on one side of the passage, and on the other a laundry with a big automatic washer, some porcelain sinks and a cabinet type deep freeze that would have taken a whole ox. She turned a key and the heavy back door protested as she pulled it open, then warm air enveloped us as we emerged into the garden.

She led me down a steep path that eventually curved its way between a couple of cedars. When we were standing in the shade beneath the low branches she said, 'This is where my husband was, Mr Lomax.'

I looked back at the house. It was built into the side of the hill and the basement came out of the ground to make it three storeys high at the rear. I worked out the window Estelle Bergman had said she'd seen her husband from. It certainly commanded a clear view of the garden, but it was no small distance away, and her sight would have had to be pretty good for her to be one-hundred-percent certain of the identity of a figure in the dawn light.

I nodded down the slope where the path disappeared in a tangle of bushes and trees. 'Where does that lead to?'

'To the back gate. It opens onto a lane that winds round onto the main road. It's dreadfully overgrown. We've hardly ever used it.'

'Presumably your husband left that way?'

She said, 'Yes,' in her whispery little voice, and we began to walk slowly back up the garden.

When we came within the shadow of the house I glanced at my watch. It was almost three-thirty and I needed to call in at the office before five.

'I don't think there's anything else I need to ask you at the moment, Mrs Bergman. I'll come back tomorrow and begin sifting through your husband's papers if I may.'

We rounded the corner of the house. I could see the Rover parked in front of the garage. As we walked across the lawn towards it she said, 'My husband and I haven't been married long. We just live for one another; no one else. I know that sounds terribly selfish, but it's true.'

We reached the car and I turned and faced her. She looked up at me with those big green eyes, and her fragile voice was intense as she went on, 'The relationship I have with Carl is so very rare and special, Mr Lomax, I know he's alive. And you're so big and clever and strong I just know you're going to find him for me and get him out of the mess he's in.'

The weak little woman act wasn't doing my ego any harm; maybe she'd not heard about women's lib. I felt ten years younger as I slid behind the wheel. The seat was hot and the interior of the car was like an oven.

'I promise you I'll do my best, Mrs Bergman. It would be wrong of me to promise more than that,' I said.

4

I headed back to Barfield. A fifteen minute struggle with the home-bound commuters got me to the market place where I parked the Rover in its usual spot. I took Carl Bergman's document case, locked the car, then began to trudge up the gentle rise that takes me past the delicatessen and across the pedestrianised area linking the parish church with a row of Georgian town houses that have been converted into offices. I've got a some-what precarious leasehold interest in a couple of attic rooms. Sometimes I feel an intruder amongst the old established firms of accountants and solicitors entrenched up here beside the church.

I climbed the worn entrance steps, crossed the lobby and looked through Melody's reception window. Melody Brown owns and manages a typing and duplicating agency that takes up most of the ground floor. On a friendly and strictly no charge basis, she does my typing, keeps an eye on the office and takes phone calls when I'm out, which is most of the time. Three or four girls were pecking away at the keys of some big electric typewriters. Melody was clipping a stencil onto the roller of a duplicator. Eventually she got it the way she wanted it, tore off some backing paper and cranked the handle a few times to pull the ink through. I watched and admired the action; Melody's I mean, not the duplicator's.

I slipped through the door and came up behind her across some apple-green cord carpeting. The typewriters were giving out a steady patter and she hadn't heard me. Her curves were doing some interesting things to a scarlet silk blouse and cream skirt. When she turned and faced me I realised the blouse wasn't the kind of thing she'd have worn at the vicar's garden party. It shouldn't have been allowed in that heat. A wave of shoulder length blonde hair had fallen over her eyes. She brushed it away with the back of her hand. I figured the vicar might not care for the scarlet nails and lips either, and the incredibly high heels on the sandals would have been the last straw. But I wasn't complaining.

Baby blue eyes raked over me and the lips pulled into a smile when she noticed the document case. 'Changing our image now, are we?'

'Just as soon as you can press my pin-stripes and dust-off the bowler hat.'

'I do too much for you already,' she snorted.

A girl with a weight problem glanced up at that, but she didn't stop pecking away at the keys.

'Any messages?' I asked.

'A few. You'd better come into the back office.'

She took me into her inner sanctum. I flopped down in the visitor's chair; she picked up a pad from beside the extension phone I'd had installed.

'Your garage phoned. Someone called Stan said if you don't pay for the last two jobs within the week he's going to give the bills to a debt collection agency.' She raised delicately arched eyebrows a millimetre, flicked over the page, then went on, 'And if you don't clear your overdraft your bank manager's going to foreclose on your car loan. He sounded really upset,' she said severely.

I nodded. I'd a pretty good idea he'd ruined his career prospects when he gave me the loan in the first place.

'Anything else?' I asked.

'Isn't that enough to be going on with?' She was perched on the edge of the desk, a pair of nicely rounded knees visible beneath the hem of her skirt.

Her curiosity seemed to get the better of her. 'Why the document case? It's not like you to carry one of those things.'

'It belongs to a client,' I said.

'You mean you actually have a client?' She injected mock surprise into her voice. Her smile was parting her lips now. Her teeth were very white.

I nodded. 'Resides up on Mount St Joseph. Lady by the name of Bergman.' I lifted the battered document case. 'This is what we in the profession refer to as a clue,' I said airily, and grinned up at her.

She threw back her head and laughed.

It was a soft, throaty sound: sunlight and warm honey.

Just sitting there and looking at her was taking too much out of me in that heat. I pushed myself out of the chair and said, 'If there are no more messages I'll head for home and maybe come back later and work an hour when it's cooler.'

'So you're on flexitime now,' she said reprovingly. 'Soon we won't see you at all.'

'You won't see me in the morning,' I said, 'I'm visiting Mrs Bergman. Should be in after lunch, though.'

'If she's made it to Mount St Joseph I suppose she's fat, blue rinsed and into her second face lift.'

I shook my head. 'She's about five-five tall, weighs a hundred and twenty pounds, give or take a few, about thirty, big green eyes, copper-gold hair . . .'

'I hope you're just as observant with all your clients,' she interrupted frostily.

I could tell she hadn't liked the idea of my having the glamorous Mrs Bergman on the books. For some reason I couldn't be bothered putting my finger on, that pleased me.

I gave her a long slow wink and said, 'See you,' then strolled out of the office. I heard her note pad thud against the door as I pulled it shut.

I went up to my office on the second floor before I left the building, clattered over the brown linoleum in the waiting room and unlocked the inner door. The place had been shut up too long. It smelt of old desk, dusty threadbare carpet, ancient papers, and plastic upholstery that had been baking in the heat. I slid the document case under the knee hole of the desk and walked straight out. Even the government surplus beechwood chairs in the waiting room seemed shabbier that afternoon. I made a mental note to change the tattered copies of Autocar that were stacked on a plastic coffee table. The pictures of Morris Oxfords and Standard Eights on the covers were a dead give-away. Maybe those issues were collectors' items now.

* * *

The sky had darkened perceptibly by the time I reached home. I parked the Rover on the crazed concrete hardstanding in front of the garage and went into the bungalow. The rumble of distant thunder didn't surprise me; a storm had been building up all afternoon and the heat and humidity were tropical.

Apart from a couple of dainty ham sandwiches I'd had at Mrs Bergman's place after the funeral, I'd not eaten all day. I fried a couple of rashers and an egg, then ate it out of the pan in a kitchen that made a shower cubicle seem spacious and probably contravened every hygiene standard in the book.

Everything felt gritty and stifling, pervaded by the apocalyptic gloom that precedes summer storms. I fixed myself a Scotch and took it with me into the bathroom. I relaxed in the tub, sipping the drink and soaking away the dust and grime of the day.

A couple more drinks later I decided not to return to the office that evening. For one thing it hadn't got any cooler; for another, wearing a bathrobe and lounging amongst the clutter of my own sitting room seemed to be the sensible thing to do with a storm coming on.

I don't know whether it was the storm or the phone that woke me. Thunder was rumbling closer and the shrilling phone was just audible above the sound of the rain. I managed to grab the handset before the ringing stopped and gave my name and number.

'Thank God. I thought you'd never answer. Come and help me. Please, please come and help me.' Her voice was tearful, hysterical almost. The line was bad, but I could tell who it was.

'What's the trouble, Mrs Bergman?'

'They've brought Carl back. They're hitting him. I've got out of the house but they're looking for me.'

'Who's brought your husband back, Mrs Bergman?'

'Some men. Three men. They're just animals. They're killing him and they're searching for me. Come. Don't ask any more questions. Just come.' She was sobbing into the phone now. What self-control she had left seemed to be ebbing away fast.

'Where are you?'

'I'm in a phone box about half-way down the Mount, but I can't stay here or they'll see me. There's a house for sale nearby. I'll hide round the back. Just come quickly,' she sobbed. The line went dead.

5

I drove as fast as I dared; twice as fast as I should. The rainfall was breaking all records and the wipers weren't clearing the screen. I seemed to be driving towards the centre of the storm. Up ahead, lightning skittered around the sky and thunder snarled and growled like some gigantic beast.

I checked the dashboard clock as I turned into the narrow road that wound up Mount St Joseph. The drive over had taken no more than ten minutes. A cloudburst had turned the road into a river. I kept in second gear, revved the engine hard and forged on up against the flow. Streetlamps were few and faint. I had the lights on full beam, but it was like driving into a black waterfall.

The estate agent's 'For Sale' board was leaning over the wall of a house about half-way up the hill. I swung the car hard into the driveway, accelerated through to the back, then cut the lights and motor. I climbed out. The rain soaked me to the skin before I'd taken a couple of steps. I couldn't hear a thing above the racket of the storm and the air was charged with the smell of warm earth soaking up the rain.

I moved out across the sodden grass, stumbling over flower beds. A haze of lightning filled the sky; the thunderclap was deafening and simultaneous. I saw her face then, in that flickering light, pale and ghostlike, watching me through the window of a tumbledown shed. I cleared some bushes and squelched towards it. She ducked out of sight, but when I pushed open the door I could see her crouching amongst the clutter of discarded junk.

'Mrs Bergman.' I spoke her name hoping the sound of my voice would identify me.

'Oh thank God it's you.' She flung herself at me, clung to my chest, shivering. 'I was so scared,' she whimpered, 'I thought it was them. I thought they'd found me.'

She turned her face up to me. It was no more than a blurred outline in the darkness. Her voice rose in strength and pitch as she said, 'You've got to go and stop them, Mr Lomax. They're in the house now. They want the book and Carl won't tell them where it is and they're murdering him.'

In some far recess of my mind a tiny voice kept asking me why she hadn't called the police, and what was I doing in a potting shed in the back yard of a house in the best part of town on a night like this. She pressed against me harder: a slender, wet bundle that was shaking with fear. I didn't bother listening to the inner voice. I just said, 'I'll put you in the car, then I'll go up to the house. Can you drive?'

She nodded dumbly.

'Then I'll leave the engine running and you can move off if things go wrong.' I draped my jacket over her shoulders: the thing was so wet it was a futile gesture. I put my arm around her and led her out into the night and the rain and the safety of the car.

★ ★ ★

I came up to the Bergman's place by way of the narrow back lane. I climbed the wall and scrambled my way up through the overgrown area at the bottom of the garden. I reached the place where I'd stood with Mrs Bergman a dozen hours earlier: the place where she claimed she'd seen her husband. I crouched beneath the branches, looking up at the house through the veil of torrential rain. Light shone from every window and the back door leading into the basement was open.

I didn't see any signs of movement in the house or garden. Thunder began to work itself up to a fresh crescendo, and I took advantage of it to sprint up the slope and reach the back of the house. I glanced through the laundry window. The light was on but the place was empty. Some of the contents of the big deep-freeze had been scattered over the floor.

I moved quickly into the basement. I stopped by the boiler room, listening. The only sounds were those of the pouring rain and my own laboured breathing. I eased the door open with my foot, waited a few seconds, then reached round the jamb and flicked on the light. A rusty sectional boiler, sprouting pipes and dials, and a heap of anthracite, filled the place. I grabbed an iron bar from beside the boiler and climbed the stone steps to the upper ground floor.

I paused again behind the door at the top of the steps. The sound of the storm was fainter here. The stairs leading up to the first floor were right above me, but the old timbers weren't whispering any secrets. I opened the door a crack and peered into the brightly lit kitchen. I couldn't see anyone, so I pushed the door open wide. The room was silent and empty.

I stepped into the kitchen. Through an open doorway I could see clear into the hall. I stood there for a while, listening to the sound of my own breathing, the iron bar gripped less tightly in my hand now. As I padded down the hall I craned my neck and glanced up the stairs. The lighting up there was dim compared to the kitchen, but good enough to tell there was no one lurking in the shadows.

I turned into the sitting room. Brown velvet curtains had been drawn across the huge bay window that looked over the front. The room had been worked over; systematically but not too violently. Books were scattered over the floor, a chair lay on its side and the doors of the rosewood sideboard hung open, the contents strewn across the carpet. The silk shade of a standard lamp was cocked at a drunken angle. I crossed the hall, opened a door on the other side and pressed a switch. Wall lamps cast a soft glow over an inch thick plate glass dining table and some brass framed chairs. It didn't seem to have been disturbed.

Thunder still rattled the windows and the rain made an incessant drumming, but I heard no sounds that might have been made inside that massively built old house. Feeling more confident, I headed up the stairs and took the doors around the landing one by one.

The bathroom was big, blue and luxuriously shiny. Enough towels to stock a department store were folded over the gold plated rails that matched the gold plated taps and gold plated shower valve. It smelt of warm dry cloth and expensive perfumes. I moved on to the master bedroom. Someone had really turned it over. The elegant wardrobes yawned open and suits and dresses had been dragged out and dumped on the floor. The bed looked like a stall at a vicarage jumble sale. Except I'm pretty sure the kind of silk and lace items that were heaped up there don't usually find their way onto stalls at jumble sales.

Carl Bergman's office was much the same. The brochures and cards which had been so neatly stacked in the nest of metal drawers were littered over the floor. Desk drawers had been pulled out, their contents scattered.

Three other sparsely furnished bedrooms didn't seem to have been touched. The suitcases, trunks and packing cases stacked in a boxroom were no more untidy than I'd have expected.

All the heat of that long summer's day seemed to be trapped up there. I felt warm despite my rain-soaked clothes. Still clutching the iron bar, and glad I'd not had to try and use it, I headed on down the stairs.

When I got back to the car she was gripping the wheel as though it was the handrail of a ship in a storm tossed sea. Her teeth were chattering.

She shoved open the door when she saw me and slid over into the passenger seat. 'Where's Carl? Why haven't you brought Carl?' she demanded.

I climbed inside, pulled the door shut against the pouring rain and faced her. 'They've gone,' I said. 'The house is empty. Maybe when they realised you'd sneaked out they got scared and took your husband away with them.'

Her body sagged when I said that. She put her hands on top of the dash and rested her forehead on them. I laid my hand on her arm while I tried to think of something to say.

She shook it off angrily. 'You're useless,' she sobbed. 'He was there and they were hurting him and you let them take him away. If I were a man I'd have

45

done better than that.' Her voice was a mixture of fear and bitterness.

I didn't say any more then, it would only have made things worse. I just left her to sob out her grief and disappointment while I drove up the hill and parked outside her front door.

She lifted her head and slumped back in the seat, her arms and hands limp by her side. 'What are you going to do?' she asked. Her voice was flat and quiet now.

'Take you inside so you can change into dry clothes and pack a few things. You can't stay alone in the house until this business is cleared up. And we've got to talk about calling the police.'

'No,' she said firmly. 'I don't want the police. Carl wouldn't like it.'

'Carl's not in any position to argue.' I said. 'You can't let hoodlums beat him up and turn your house over and not call the police.'

'It might seem like that to you, Mr Lomax, but I'm telling you, I don't want the police involved. Carl sometimes got information for his articles in ways the police wouldn't approve: using false names, mixing with criminals, things like that. And there are other reasons . . . '

'Other reasons?'

'All part of his having to come to England.'

I could tell from the tone of her voice that she wanted the conversation to end there, so I just insisted, 'But you will let me take you away from the house. I can't let you stay there alone.'

She sighed, and her voice was a surrender to defeat as she said bitterly, 'Yes, Mr Lomax. I'll let you take me away from my home.'

I climbed out of the car, walked round and opened the passenger door. She slid those long legs out and made her way up the front steps to the massive entrance. Even with her hair and summer dress saturated by the storm, and with my shabby jacket draped over her shoulders, she still managed a kind of quiet dignity. She strode on into the house, straight backed and with the kind of feline assurance the fashion magazines call poise.

Without saying another word to me she

walked down the hall and began climbing the stairs. I went through to the kitchen, then down to the basement and closed and bolted the back door. When I went into the laundry to douse the light I saw the frozen food they'd scattered over the floor. I heaved up the lid of the massive freezer; a wave of coolness drifted past me. I gathered up the bags and cartons and heaped them on top of the ones inside. I guess I should have been more careful because when I dropped the lid it wouldn't quite shut. I spread the packages more carefully. When I lowered it again I put my weight behind it, felt the rubber seals squeeze tight and heard the lock click. I climbed up to the kitchen, killed the lights, and strode on into the hall. Back in the sitting room, I dragged the big armchair upright, straightened the crazy shade on the standard lamp and stacked books on some shelves in an alcove. Then I flopped down on the chesterfield, allowed my eyelids to droop while I waited for Mrs Bergman. The storm had worn itself out now, and the birds had begun to greet the day.

'Mr Lomax.'

I jerked upright. I must have been dozing. Estelle Bergman was looking down at me. She'd dried her hair and drawn it back rather severely from her face. The crisp white dress was doing its best to make her look brand new again, but the lipstick, powder and eyeshadow couldn't conceal the deathly sadness in her face.

'I'm sorry I spoke to you the way I did, Mr Lomax,' she said softly. 'None of this is your fault. You got here as quickly as you could.'

I prised myself up from the chesterfield. 'Don't even think about it,' I said. 'I've checked the place over and doused all the lights. I think we should get you out of here now.'

She nodded, crossed over to the bay window and drew the velvet curtains back. The sky was just becoming light. We went into the hall. I gathered up the red leather suitcase she'd left at the foot of the stairs and led the way out to the car. I helped her into the passenger seat and put her case in the back. Then I locked the front door and got myself behind the wheel.

'There's a motel about ten miles north of town. What if I book you in there? It's anonymous: if anyone comes searching for you again it's probably the last place they'd look.'

'Anywhere will do, Mr Lomax. Just anywhere.' Resignation and sadness mingled in the cold, quiet voice.

I started the car and pointed it down the hill. The sun had climbed the horizon in the east, silhouetting the church spires and tower blocks of council flats over in Barfield. Roofs, roads and vegetation were glistening wet after the rain.

'Do you think they found the book?' I asked.

'Who knows what the brutes found?'

'How did you manage to get away?'

'They were trying to get Carl to tell them where the book was. He kept saying he didn't know. I've never seen men so big and angry and ugly as that before: they had stockings pulled over their heads. It made them look unreal and utterly terrifying. Then they started threatening to hurt me if he didn't get them the book. The things they said were unspeakable.' She shuddered. 'Carl just went wild then, and they started hitting him. I managed to slip out of the house while it was all going on and I ran down the hill and phoned you.'

When I booked her into the motel I caught sight of myself in a mirrored panel behind the reception desk. I looked as though I'd been under a bursting dam. The guy at the desk didn't notice. He couldn't drag his eyes off Mrs Bergman. Even after that traumatic, sleepless night she could still have made a Salvation Army major kick a hole in his drum.

I carried her bag to a room that was just like fifty others: small, neat, clean and with no more character than a concrete bus shelter.

'Thank you for bringing me, Mr Lomax.'

'Try and get some sleep,' I said. 'And when you wake have lunch.'

Her manner had undergone a subtle change. She seemed detached and distant, just as she had been at the graveside.

But now a deathly calm, a kind of defeated resignation, overlaid it all.

'I'll grab a shave and change my clothes,' I said. 'Then I'll try and get a lead on who these people are, and where they've taken your husband.'

She shook her head. It was a barely perceptible movement. 'I'm pretty sure you're wasting your time now, Mr Lomax.'

I raised an eyebrow.

'You don't think I'd have let you take me away from the house if I thought there was a chance of Carl coming back, do you? Nothing would have induced me to leave. As I told you, we were very close to one another. So close that my whole being is telling me he's gone now. They've killed him, Mr Lomax. I just know they have.'

'Why should they kill him?' I asked. 'Especially if they haven't found what they were looking for.'

She sighed wearily. 'It's something I feel.'

'You're exhausted,' I said. 'When you've had some sleep and a meal you'll maybe think differently.'

'Whether my feelings are right or wrong, Mr Lomax, I want you to find those men for me. I won't rest until the dirty animals are caught.'

6

I picked up the solitary bottle of milk, pulled the daily ration of gloom and doom from the letter box, and stepped into the bungalow. The place felt empty and uncared for, but the smell of the meal I'd cooked the night before was there to greet me like a faint and vaguely unpleasant memory. I didn't linger; just washed, shaved, changed my clothes. I locked up, got behind the wheel of the Rover and weaved my way back through the estate. The main Barfield road was clogged solid with commuters. I eased the car out with a cheeky determination and caught the angry blare of a dozen horns before a guy in a yellow Volkswagen weakened and let me join the convoy.

I had to endure the eight-thirty stop-start routine all the way into Barfield. I whiled away the time by mulling over the events of the past twenty-four hours, trying to impose some order on the chaos. When I'd checked over the Bergman residence not all of the rooms had been disturbed. and there was no sign of the villains or the husband. Maybe when they realised Mrs Bergman had crept out they decided to scarper. Or maybe Carl Bergman wilted under the beating and told them where his notebook was. I got to thinking the damage they'd done wasn't all that bad. Most places that are broken into and worked over look as though they've been hit by the demolition man's flying ball. A few chairs had been up-ended in the sitting room, but it didn't look as if anyone had been beaten to death in there. And she'd seemed determined not to let me go to the police, even with her husband abducted by four gorillas who wore stocking masks while they kicked hell out of him and smashed up the happy home. I couldn't accept she'd be that worried about the way he collected information for his articles, or any irregularities surrounding their coming to England. Maybe she couldn't face the humiliation of another rejection by some doubting chief inspector. Or perhaps it was the truth she couldn't face . . .

I began to wonder if the whole thing was a put up job. Maybe the shock of sudden bereavement, the loss of someone she was totally besotted with really had affected her mind. Perhaps her first response had been to completely reject the fact of his death and from then on she'd fabricated events to support her in the belief that her husband was still alive. The bite mark on his chest, his dawn visit to the garden, even to turning out the freezer and one or two drawers last night while the storm raged. Maybe when she'd told me at the motel that she now felt her husband was dead, she was taking her first step along the road to reality and an acceptance of the truth.

When I had to leap on the brakes to save myself the price of a three-figure bodywork job I realised I was giving too much attention to the Bergman business. As I made a right into the market place I reminded myself it was a private investigator she'd said she needed. Who was I to argue? If she'd wanted a trick-cyclist she'd have found one. I parked the car and made my way up the rise to the office.

I gathered the mail from the box behind my slot and thumbed through it while I climbed the stairs. I crossed the waiting room, unlocked the inner door, slid the window open and got behind the desk. I began to open the envelopes: a cheque that wouldn't do much for the bank overdraft, a call to give evidence at a court hearing, a final rate demand and a bill for some new stationery. I pocketed the cheque and stacked the rest on a new pile I was starting alongside the telephone. The sudden flurry of activity sent a spider legging it for cover across the blotter.

I relaxed back in the chair. I figured the office was as good a place as any to catch up on the lost shut-eye. When I stretched out, my foot contacted the Bergman briefcase and I remembered I'd slid it under the knee hole the day before.

I reached down and hoisted it up onto the desk, slid the catches back and got the thing open. I tipped Carl Bergman's photograph, the odds and ends in the plastic bag, the newspaper and the rest of the stuff onto the blotter and groped around in the pockets in the lid. They were all empty. The suede lining seemed to be glued to the metal shell. I checked the depth against the outside measurement. There was no hidden compartment.

I pocketed the photograph and the bunch of keys from the bag, then I glanced down at the tightly folded copy of the Barfield Echo. I opened it out and leafed through the pages. A late edition, it was dated about three weeks before Carl Bergman or some other guy got roasted in the burning car. The tail end of the small ad's section gets very personal in the Echo. I ran my eye down the columns. Attractive, lonely hearted widows willing to pay their way. Divorcees with good figures looking for good times and widowers, boasting their own hair and teeth, dying to give it to them. Clean living car owning young men seeking nubile partners, holiday partners, even life-time partners. Barfield's ragged army of walking wounded all trying to grab a little consolation.

One item made me linger. A faint scribble of pencil marked it off from the others. It read: 'Cleo is dressed for dancing and waiting for Anthony in the Garden of Eden'.

I got my brogues up and tried to figure out what it might mean, but that morning tiredness was making the usual low IQ problem even worse. I was busy getting nowhere when I heard high-heels tapping over the linoleum in the outer office, the rattle of crockery as the connecting door opened. I kept my eyes shut, my fingers laced on my chest.

'And how's Barfield's super sleuth today?'

Melody's astringent comments don't often cut through to a nerve, but the sleepless night was making me edgy. I heard her lower the tray onto the desk and caught the aroma of freshly ground coffee. I opened one eye slowly, then got the other open fast. Dressed up the way she was that morning I'd have forgiven her anything: frilly pink blouse pulled tight in all the right places, blonde hair bouncing around on her shoulders, pearly pink lipstick. I dragged my feet off the desk and made a grab for the cup.

'How do you always know what I want?' I asked gratefully.

'I've a pretty good idea what you need,' she said. 'I wouldn't dare hazard a guess at what you want.'

I couldn't figure that one out, so I just let it ride.

She pushed aside a heap of papers, clapped the dust from her hands and perched on the edge of the desk. 'We are looking a little fragile this morning,' she said brightly.

I took another sip of the coffee and bit into a slice of toast. I nodded sleepily. 'It's all the sleuthing,' I said. 'I had to work the night shift. Mrs Bergman thought some guys in stocking masks were chasing her and she called me out.'

Melody sniffed. From under long, curving lashes the blue eyes were giving me a look that mingled disapproval and suspicion in about equal proportions.

'She must have been pretty desperate,' she said, working hard at a couldn't-care-less voice.

I swallowed another mouthful of the coffee and attacked the second slice of toast. 'She was scared half-to-death,' I said.

'Big men?' she said.

I nodded while I chewed. I can just manage to do both at once.

'In stocking masks?'

I nodded some more.

The lips pouted to kill the smile. 'I'd have thought she could have dreamt up something a little less corny.'

'She was genuine,' I protested.

Melody sighed and gave me her long-suffering look.

'But I can't work out whether it's all for real or whether it's some fantasy she's weaving to convince herself her husband's still alive,' I went on.

I handed her the copy of the Barfield Echo, pointed to the marked ad' and said, 'What do you make of that?'

She frowned at it for a few seconds before she said, 'There's a dress shop called The Garden of Eden. In Greyfriar's Walk off the bottom of High Street. Very exclusive. In fact I'd say it's Barfield's best.'

61

'Thanks. But what's the 'Cleo's dressed for dancing and waiting for Anthony' all about?'

'Probably just advertising,' she said. 'Restaurants often slip a disguised ad' in the personal columns.'

'But surely not some classy dress shop?'

She shrugged. 'Who knows? Why shouldn't the kind of place women like your Mrs Bergman get their dresses and unmentionables from do a little advertising?'

'She's not my Mrs Bergman,' I retorted. I didn't tell her I'd seen most of Mrs Bergman's flimsy underwear heaped up on the bed the night before. I'd have been kissing the coffee and tea goodbye for a month, maybe forever. But I smiled at the recollection.

She smiled back, warmly this time, so she couldn't have guessed what I was thinking. She stood up, moved round to the front of the desk and gathered the crockery onto the tray.

We looked at one another across the clutter of papers for what seemed like quite a while, then she pulled a handkerchief from the sleeve of her blouse: a square inch of linen stitched to a square foot of lace.

She leant forward. 'You've got butter in your dimple,' she said, and began to dab my chin. The perfume on the ridiculous handkerchief was expensive and restrained; not the kind of thing you'd catch the local rugger team wearing, even in Barfield. It wouldn't have bored me if she'd kept up the treatment all morning. And then she'd picked up the tray and moved off towards the door.

'Thanks for the coffee and toast,' I called after her.

'I can't think why I bother,' she said. 'You certainly don't deserve it.'

I'd got my feet back up on the desk before she cleared the outer office, and I was making good the lost sleep before she reached the bottom of the stairs.

★   ★   ★

The grimy town hall clock was showing five-past-two. I crossed the road, weaving

63

between the streams of slow moving traffic, then headed down the side of a department store that took up a whole block. I rounded the front of the store. It opened onto High Street. Another fifty paces and I entered Greyfriar's Walk, a narrow lane no more than twelve feet wide.

On either side old houses had been converted into smart little shops: the kind of select places that specialise in expensive baubles for people who already have more than they need but still haven't got everything they want. I strolled past a milliner's and a window full of shoes and handbags, then saw the place called The Garden of Eden sandwiched between a jeweller's and a coffee house. The Georgian style shop front was painted white and gold. Dresses were displayed on black manikins. They carried price tags you had to read twice to make sure you'd got it right the first time. What I took to be the figure of Eve with strategic fig leaves had been etched into the glass panel in the top half of the door. I worked the handle, then stepped inside onto black carpeting.

Dresses were hanging in arched alcoves that ran around the walls, and there were some more racks of clothes in the centre of the shop. Disco music played softly, almost drowned out by the shrill, happy chatter of the dozen young, and not so young, women who were packed into what floor space remained. At the back, changing booths were curtained off with red velvet drapes. The air was heavy with a cloying mixture of perfumes and the smell of new cloth.

I shut the door behind me and triggered off something that sounded like a peal of cow bells. No one noticed. I stood with my back to the door and did my best to look nonchalant. They were all telling one another how sweet, super and marvellous they looked, and how it was 'just you, darling'. Ripples of girlish laughter kept rising above it all. I caught an assistant's eye and she came over.

'Can I help you?' she asked. She had a baby-doll face and a high-pitched lisping voice to match. Her hair was a mass of tight, brown curls.

I got my wallet and fished out a card a

car salesman had given me a few weeks previously. I handed it to her and said, 'We're in difficulties because one of our salesmen's left us. We think he sold a car to someone who works here. The deal involved fitting a new clutch and gear box. We've got the parts now, but the carbon of the sales docket is so poor we can't make out the name, and the address is pretty indistinct.' I showed her the photo' of Carl Bergman. I'd decided against a direct approach; the item in the personal column could have been no more than a disguised advertisement and the patter about the car would enable me to exit gracefully.

Her eyes moved from my face to Bergman's photo', then back to my face again. She fluttered her lashes. 'I only work here now and again, Mr Fosdyke,' she lisped, 'but Helen, Miss Davenport that is, might be able to help. She's serving a customer now, but if you'll wait here I'll get her to come over when she's free.'

She pulled a gilded, cabriole-legged chair clear of some drapes for me. I thanked her and lowered myself onto the red velvet. She crossed the tiny, crowded shop. I could see her head and shoulders above the racks of dresses as she spoke to a taller woman who was pushing fifty hard enough to bend a girder. They glanced in my direction and the visiting card changed hands. The older woman nodded, said something I couldn't hear, then turned to a Scandinavian-looking blonde who'd just emerged from one of the changing booths.

I don't get embarrassed easily, but I was beginning to feel as conspicuous as a ham shank in a synagogue. I looked to see if the one called Helen Davenport was coming over. She was taking the dress from the blonde with the wide cheek bones. She draped it over a glass topped counter and began to fold it, placing sheets of tissue paper between the layers of material, her hands fluttering over it, teasing the cloth smooth and straight. She got a pink candy-striped bag from beneath the counter and gently slid the dress into it. The blonde handed over some notes, the Davenport woman operated a small cash register, then passed her the bag and some change. She walked with her to the door. As they came closer I could hear her telling the blonde how 'absolutely divine' and 'utterly you' the dress looked. The ego massage seemed to be an essential part of the service. She was still giving her the treatment when she opened the door for her and gushed out a goodbye.

She closed the door and set the cow bells jangling again. I rose to my feet. She came towards me with the kind of exaggerated movements fashion models make when they strut down the catwalk. She looked me over appraisingly. High-heeled shoes made her appear tall. Her slenderness was accentuated by a tight brown skirt, but she was by no means thin. She was wearing a cream blouse with very full sleeves. There were streaks of grey in her long hair which was gathered on top of her head. Her face had been carefully made-up. She'd always been some distance this side of beautiful, but turned out like that she was still an attractive woman.

She glanced at the card to check the name, then looked me straight in the eye and said, 'Can I help you, Mr Fosdyke?' Her voice was low and throaty. It was the kind of voice I always associate with too many cigarettes, or too much drink, or just too much living. It wasn't the kind of voice a young girl can ever have.

I repeated the spiel about wanting to fix a clutch and a gearbox in a car that had been sold and showed her Carl Bergman's photograph. 'That's the rep who handled the sale,' I said. 'Unfortunately he's left the firm and I'm having some difficulty tracing the customer.'

'I certainly recognise him. I saw him once or twice, waiting to pick up one of my girls. But I didn't get the impression he was selling her something; they seemed much more friendly than that.'

She handed back the photograph. I slipped it into my wallet.

'Would it be possible for me to have a word with the young lady,' I said. 'We're anxious to call the car in and do the work. The cost was included in the sale price.'

She smiled. 'It's extremely refreshing these days to find a firm that's keen to honour its obligations.'

I smiled right back. 'We aim to please, Miss Davenport.'

Bold, tawny eyes looked me up and down. 'I'm sure you do, Mr Fosdyke, I'm quite sure you do.' Her throaty voice sounded wistful.

'The young lady,' I prompted. 'Would it be possible for me to see her.'

She blinked rapidly. She seemed to be struggling to collect her thoughts. 'Er, I'm afraid not. You see, I had to let her go. About a month ago.'

'Let her go?' I repeated the euphemism.

'Ask her to leave,' she said. 'I run a very high class establishment, Mr Fosdyke. I just can't risk my girls upsetting the customers. Miss Soames began to be ill rather frequently while she was at the shop. In fact I'm putting it kindly. Sometimes her behaviour was nothing short of bizarre.'

She moved her hands expressively while she talked. Her fingers were a mass of ornate rings, and the crimson nails

70

were so long and perfect they had to be artificial.

'I'm sorry to hear that,' I said. 'May I ask in what way?'

She shrugged. 'It's difficult to say precisely. It was a kind of instability. Sometimes she'd be laughing and giggling uncontrollably. Once I found her hunched up in the stockroom, wild eyed and shivering. One of my best customers thought Miss Soames was laughing at her when she was trying on a dress. She was very upset. Stormed out of the shop. I had to ask Miss Soames to leave then.'

I nodded and tried to arrange my features in a sympathetic expression. 'Do you have Miss Soames' home address?' I asked. 'I'd like to contact her and arrange for the work to be done on her car if I can.'

She beckoned over the girl with the lisp. 'Judy, would you be a dear and get me the wages book?'

The girl weaved her way between the customers and slipped through the red velvet drapes.

The Davenport dame turned back to

me gave me a smile that was more than friendly. Her teeth were large and there were gold cappings amongst the white. She moved closer to me, put her hand on my arm and gazed at me in a blatantly provocative way. 'If you take that much trouble with your customers, Mr Fosdyke, I think I'd like you to try and find something special for me,' she said throatily. 'Something fast and sporty. I don't mind if it's been . . . how do you say . . . well run in, but I don't want anything that's worn out, if you know what I mean.'

I met her gaze without blinking and smiled right back. She was drenched in some kind of musky perfume that was a long way from the lavender water grandmother used to wear.

'I think I know what you mean, Miss Davenport, and I think I can find just what you're looking for,' I said.

The girl with the lisp came back, handed her a blue cash book then disappeared again behind the rack of dresses. Helen Davenport opened the book and flicked through it. She leant towards me, close enough for me to smell her hair, and read out an address, slowly, while I noted it down.

She snapped the book shut and smiled up at me again. Her tawny eyes held mine and the false eyelashes didn't even quiver as she said, 'I certainly hope you can get me something special. Perhaps you'll give me a ring when you've come up with something?'

'I'll certainly do that. I'll probably be in touch over the next couple of days or so.'

She took her hand off my arm and raised a finger in mock admonition. 'Don't forget now. If I've not heard from you by Monday I'll drop into the showrooms and see what you have to offer.'

'I'll look forward to that,' I said. 'And don't worry, I'm sure we'll be able to find something just right for you.'

She pulled the door open. Her eyes ranged over me hungrily, one last time. 'I'm not worrying, Mr Fosdyke. I've every confidence you'll get me just what I need.'

There was no answer to that. I stepped

through the door and headed back towards the place where I'd parked the car. It was a long time since I'd been propositioned by a woman who was even remotely attractive. Thinking about it, I couldn't remember when I'd last been propositioned by any woman. Fosdyke was about five feet three, fat, bald and over sixty. For all I knew he was happily married. I figured they were both in for a surprise if Helen Davenport kept her promise and turned up at the showrooms on Monday.

7

The address Helen Davenport had given me was for a council flat in one of the high rise blocks on the east side of town. I parked the car some distance away. With almost every tenant on the estate jobless, pennyless and hopeless, a nearly new three-and-a-half litre Rover might have been too much salt in sore wounds.

I climbed down into the pedestrian subway. Rough cast concrete walls had beaten the graffiti artists, but broken lights and blocked gulleys made the place a gloomy tunnel almost ankle deep in oily water. I groped my way up the steps on the far side and emerged into sunlight and the estate. This was the place where, rumour had it, television sets rained down from the fourteenth floor. So I kept to the hard packed earth where grass should have been, and where the splintered stumps of trees made the place look like the aftermath of the battle of the Somme.

A dozen streets of back-to-backs had gone to make way for these high rise concrete chicken coops. I couldn't figure out which was worse: the mill owners' back-to-backs or the skyscraper flats. Whichever it was, I'd a shrewd idea there wouldn't be any architects or planners bunked down in there.

I strode through the entrance door of a block nameplated Arkwright House. A smell of disinfectant masked the under-lying lavatorial odour, and a recent coat of paint had almost hidden the graffiti on the walls. I punched the lift button. Presently the scarred metal doors slid aside. I stepped into a miniscule compart-ment. A boy punk and a girl punk were grunting amorously at one another. Spiky multi-coloured hair, safety pins and chains: a careless move could have meant a lost eye. I pressed the button marked seven, the doors rolled shut like the lid sliding over a coffin, and the three of us rattled upwards.

Flat twenty-eight was at the end of the concrete access landing. I knocked on the reeded glass panel in the top half of the door and waited. There was no answer. I stepped to the edge of the access deck and peered over the waist high wall to the battlefield below, where the shadow of one twenty storey block reached out to finger the sunlit face of the next. The place felt dead and deserted. But over the low rumble of traffic on the urban freeway I caught the excited jabbering of a television sports commentator, the rattle of a dustbin lid, a slamming door.

I tapped on the glass again, hard and insistent this time. A girl's voice called, 'All right, all right, I'm coming.' I heard a toilet flush, and a few seconds later a shape moved behind the reeded glass.

She opened the door just wide enough to get her face round the edge. I don't know whether her father or her mother had been coloured. It didn't matter. The consequence was a creature of rare beauty.

'Well?' she demanded.

'Miss Soames?'

'What if it is?'

I got my wallet, pulled out the photograph of Carl Bergman and held it up for her to see.

The eyebrows lifted and the tiny, rounded chin dropped far enough to reveal perfect teeth. They were brilliant white against the smooth dark skin of her face.

'Tony,' she said. 'You want to see me about Tony?'

'I can't talk out here, Miss Soames, perhaps I could come inside.'

Suspicion chased the surprise from her face.

I took a business card from my wallet and offered it to her. Slender brown fingers plucked it out of my hand and the almond eyes gave it the once over.

'Tony's not in any trouble, is he?'

'He could be, Miss Soames. Perhaps I could come in for a moment?'

She pulled the door open wide and motioned me in with a jerk of her head. I stepped into a tiny blue and white kitchen. She closed the door, then led me across an internal hall to a small sitting room on the sunlit side of the block. She was wearing a skimpy, sleeveless yellow jumper, and the legs of her faded jeans had been torn off just below the knee, exposing her calves. She was barefoot, and a band of flesh was visible between the hem of the jumper and the waist-band of the jeans. Her arms and neck were long and slender.

She nodded towards a black plastic armchair that had cushions covered with some fluorescent-green fur. I sat down. She curled up on the matching sofa. We eyed one another across a purple shag pile carpet. On the wall above her head was a larger than life photograph of a male pop star in a cheap plastic frame.

'How did you find out where I lived?' The figure matched the face but the voice didn't. It was aggressive and hard. She had a strong Yorkshire accent.

'They told me at the shop where you used to work?' I was relieved she hadn't asked me how I'd connected her with Carl Bergman: it spared me more explanations, more lies.

'Huh,' she snorted. 'And what else did that silly old cow Davenport tell you.'

I smiled. 'I only asked her where you lived. That's all she told me.'

'Got a fag?'

I shook my head. 'I'm afraid I don't use them.'

'Have to smoke my own then.'

She stood up and shuffled over to a battered oak sideboard. She rummaged around in a red handbag that lay on its ring marked top. I heard a match striking, then she shuffled back with a king sized cigarette pressed between her lips. She curled up on the sofa again, her eyes narrowing behind the smoke.

'He's been missing about a month,' I said. 'His wife's hired me to find him.'

She exhaled smoke through her nose. 'What's she like? Mrs Maxwell, I mean.'

I shrugged. 'Like a wife,' I said evasively. At least I'd found out the name Carl Bergman used when he went on the town looking for information. I drew some satisfaction from that.

'I bet she's pretty.'

'You could say she is.'

'She'd have to be to hook a fella like that. Tony wouldn't have married anyone who wasn't.' She sighed and gave me a resigned little smile. 'All the blokes worth having are already married. If you come across a decent looking fella who's got a few quid and who knows how to treat a girl, it's an odds on cert some scheming bitch has got there first.'

'Do you know where he might be?' I figured it was time I started asking the questions.

She became thoughtful. 'Not really. Travellers roam all over the place. Could be anywhere.'

'Travellers?'

'You know,' she explained. 'Sales reps. He travelled for a drug firm. He told me he covered from Sledingborough right down to Ramford City.'

I nodded, trying to convince her I remembered that he did.

'What are his kids like?'

'Just nice, ordinary kids,' I lied.

'He told me he'd have walked out on her, but he couldn't leave three small kids. Lucky cow.'

'Why lucky?' I asked, 'when there's so much going on and she doesn't know about it?'

She gave me a defeated little smile. 'I

wouldn't have minded too much if he was mine and I'd got a piece of paper to prove it. Fellas are like that, aren't they? At least he didn't mess on his own doorstep. She's down there in Ramford City playing mummies and daddies. I just take care of him while he's up here.' She frowned, flicked ash onto the carpet before adding sadly, 'Or I used to.'

'What happened?' I asked.

She dragged at the cigarette and smoke escaped from her mouth as she said, 'I guess I lost him where I found him, at the Centre of the Galaxy.'

'Huh?'

'You know,' she said, 'the disco under the boozer in the market place.'

I nodded and said I knew where she meant. I didn't of course. I'd no idea Barfield was graced with an outfit called Centre of the Galaxy.

'Tony was just something else,' she said wistfully. 'Almost every Thursday night I'd meet him there and we'd come back here afterwards. Do you know what he used to call me?' She seemed to be completely absorbed in her reminiscences now.

I shook my head.

'Cleo. He used to call me Cleo. Once he said I was his dark, Egyptian queen of the night.' She sighed.

Her straight hair was thick and raven black. It fell to the nape of her neck. A straight fringe crossed her brow. Dark skin, almond eyes, tiny pouting mouth, all crowned by that thick mane of black hair. Cleopatra: there was no other pet name he could have given her.

'So, what went wrong?'

'I guess I always knew deep down it wouldn't last for ever. There's just too much competition. Classy fellas like that can't help spreading themselves around. One night they had a live band at the disco. There was this singer, Roxy Morningstar. You ever heard of her? I could tell she fancied Tony. They alternated the band with records. When there was dancing to records she couldn't leave him alone. I never really saw him again after that. Not properly, if you know what I mean. Someone told me they'd seen him at the Wetherton Country Club. She sings there. I wish the rotten cow had stayed there instead of slumming it at the disco.'

'Wasn't Tony a bit old for the disco?'

She shrugged. With her shoulders it was an eloquent gesture. 'He was older than most of us, but he was a great dancer and he fitted in okay. Anyway, being a sales rep for a medical company made him popular.'

'How was that?'

She gave me a pitying look. 'For the sweets,' she said. 'You could always cadge a few from him?'

'Sweets?'

'You know: Dexies, Bennies, French Blues, that sort of thing.'

'You mean drugs?'

'Sure. Something to keep you up right through the weekend. You can get most things at the disco if you know who to ask, but Tony was always good for a Dexy or a Benny.'

'Most things?'

'Sure. Pot, horse, snow. But I've never seen any acid passed around there.'

'Horse? Snow?'

She smiled and gave me the pitying

look again. 'Heroin and cocaine,' she said. 'You don't see a lot of that about though. Mostly it's just amphetamines, something to give you a lift and keep you on a high. That's all Tony ever gave away. I never saw him with any stuff.'

'Why do you think he spread the sweets around like that?'

'He was just a great fella,' she said. 'You know, fun to be with. Anyway, he didn't spread them around. Just gave a few to the chicks who were into that scene.'

'But what about the guys who were in there trying to sell the things? Didn't they get mad when he started handing them out for free?'

She blew smoke towards the ceiling and laughed throatily. 'It wasn't like that,' she said. 'He only gave them to me and two or three other kids. Anyway, Tony got friendly with the dealers and there was no hassle. He was just a great fella. Everybody liked him.'

'Why do you think he got acquainted with the people who sell the stuff?'

Her eyes narrowed. She stabbed the end of her cigarette into a chipped glass ashtray balanced on the arm of the sofa. 'You sure you're just trying to find him for his wife?' she asked suspiciously. 'I don't see what all of this has got to do with finding him.'

'That's all I'm trying to do, Miss Soames. Find him. I'm not from the police, if that's what's worrying you. It's none of my business what he's been doing, or what anyone else has been doing for that matter. All I'm looking for is something that will lead me to him.'

She didn't speak, just went on eyeing me suspiciously.

'He could be in big trouble,' I said gently. 'I know I've been hired by his wife, but if you ever felt anything for him you ought to tell me what you know. It could be important.'

She seemed to retreat farther into the sofa. She frowned thoughtfully, then said, 'It was none of my business, but I did wonder if he was trying to muscle in on things. Supply the dealers, something like that. He seemed to want to know all about the local drugs scene. And that singing bitch Roxy Morningstar who got her claws in him, everybody knows she's shooting horse and snow.'

I raised an eyebrow.

She gave an exasperated little snort. 'Speedball,' she said. 'Heroin and cocaine. You get a hell of a buzz with a cocktail like that. But I've never tried it; in fact I've finished with the whole scene.' She smiled pityingly, then added, 'You know, for a private investigator you seem pretty thick.'

'That's why I've got to ask so many stupid questions,' I said. 'Did he leave any clothes or papers here?'

'Not a thing. He never really stayed here. He always went back to his hotel before morning. He said he didn't want the neighbours gossiping about me. Most guys wouldn't have cared, but he did.'

'When did you last see him?'

'About six weeks ago. When that bitch Morningstar started chasing him. I tried to get in touch, I suppose I wanted to tell him what had happened, but he never told me where he lived in Ramford, so it was no use.'

'Happened?'

She sighed, gave me a tight-lipped

smile. 'I'm expecting his kid, aren't I? That's why I've packed in the speed, cut the fags down to one or two a day. Don't want the kid hurt, do I?'

The smile hadn't reached her eyes. They were telling me she was worried and scared. All the bravado couldn't hide the fact she was just a frightened kid: used, deserted, alone.

'When did you leave the dress shop?'

'I didn't leave. I was sacked, wasn't I?' she said. 'About three weeks ago. I was feeling pretty bad about Tony, so I rolled myself a joint and smoked it in the carsi. When I went back in the shop I had to serve this fat old bag who wanted an evening gown. I couldn't stop giggling. Pot makes you like that sometimes. Stupid old cow thought I was laughing at her and stormed out. Davenport sacked me on the spot.'

We eyed one another for a few moments. I couldn't fault Carl Bergman's taste. He could certainly pick the lookers. But this one had been busy trading health and vitality for fleeting pleasure. She was probably at her best now. By the time she was thirty, too many good times and not enough good food, too little sleep and too much of the stuff she called speed would leave her looking used and old.

I stood up and said, 'Thanks for talking to me, Miss Soames. You've been a great help.'

'It's okay,' she said. 'Just give him my love when you find him.'

I stepped over to the window. Staring down at the Dinky cars almost gave me vertigo. 'You've got quite a view,' I said.

'It's better at night, when all the lights come on,' she said. 'You can see right across town to Mount St Joseph. When its clear the lights in the houses there seem to get mixed up with the stars.'

I turned and faced her. She was standing right behind me, her slender arms folded beneath her breasts.

'But you can't see as far south as Ramford City,' I said softly.

She laughed. There was no bitterness in the sound, just acceptance. 'No, Mr Lomax, I guess I can't see that far. Not even from up here.'

8

I got back to the office building a few minutes before five. I didn't bother climbing the stairs to my own attic rooms. I just went straight into Melody's agency. The girls were pulling dust covers over their machines, getting ready to quit for the day. I walked on through and found Melody behind a tidy desk. She looked as cool and fresh as she had that morning. She was making entries in a cash book.

I flopped down in the visitor's chair and stretched out. The gritty heat of the day, the noise and fumes of the traffic, the meanness of the high rise flats and Carl Bergman's grubby little lies had got to me. I felt weary and somehow diminished by it all.

'Any messages?' I asked.

She capped the elegant tortoise-shell pen and laid it in its place on the desk stand. Her glossy pink lips were pressed together in a firm line and the blue eyes seemed concerned. She looked like a nurse who's been sent to tell the concert pianist he's going to have a hand amputated.

She sighed, gave me a wry smile, then said, 'The Telecom men have been: I'm afraid they've cut your phone off. The man at the garage who calls himself Stan sent a debt collector round this afternoon, a great smelly brute. Your bank manager phoned: he's had instructions to start court proceedings if you've not cleared your overdraft by Friday.'

I relaxed deeper into the chair and grinned at her across the desk. 'Now give me the really bad news.'

'Don't you ever worry about anything?' she protested.

'Only the things I can do something about.'

I don't know whether I was trying to fool Melody or myself when I said that. Deep down I was as worried as hell. Everything seemed to be going to pieces. I was owed a good deal of money by some pretty big outfits, but firms like that don't rush to pay.

'Anything else?'

'Mrs Bergman phoned. She wants you to call her as soon as you can. She said you'd know how to get hold of her.'

My grin widened.

'And that's something you don't need me to tell you,' she said.

'I'm not with you,' I lied.

'How to get hold of her. Just follow your instincts, you'll get along fine.'

I laughed gently. 'Ever been to the Wetherton Country Club?' I was trying to jump the conversation onto fresh tracks.

'No, but I'll bet Mrs Bergman has. It's the kind of place I imagine she'd get taken to.'

'Pretty high class, I suppose?'

'So I'm told.'

'Maybe the members just like to think so,' I said. 'Perhaps its the universal brotherhood of wealth rather than the bonds of class.'

'I know you're having difficulties,' she said primly, 'but there's no need for you to get bitter and twisted.'

I prised myself out of the chair and grinned down at her. 'I guess you're right,' I said. 'It's just the way the cookie crumbles.' I strolled out of her office and weaved my way between the desks towards the door.

The church clock was chiming five when I emerged into the bright, sticky heat again. While I headed down the slope to the spot where I'd parked the car my thoughts turned to Mrs Bergman and her villa up on Mount St Joseph, to the Soames girl in her concrete chicken coop on the east side of town. The two women didn't have anything in common. Unless, that is, you count stunning good looks and a part share in Carl Bergman, alias Tony Maxwell. And just how small a share I'd yet to find out.

★   ★   ★

When I left the office I motored out to the Bergman residence. I parked the car half way along the road that winds up Mount St Joseph. I moved in the back way, over the wall and through the overgrown shrubbery at the bottom of the garden.

I stopped before I left the shadow of the trees, just short of the spot where Mrs Bergman said she'd seen her husband. I stared up at the house. Red brick and grimy stone. Fretted barge boards rode the steep roofs: painted white they were like lace trimming on an old woman's bonnet. The windows stared back at me: dark, shiny, inscrutable. I waited, listened to birds warbling and bees droning: the music of summer. The house didn't make a sound. After a couple of minutes I came out from under the trees, made my way up the steeply sloping lawn and round to the front door.

I rang the bell a few times and waited, just to be sure I had the place to myself. No one answered. I let myself in with one of the keys on the bunch I'd taken from Carl Bergman's case. The size of the place, the massive walls, meant it was cooler inside. I went through and down and checked the rear door in the semi-basement. It was all just the way I'd left it during the early hours of that morning.

I climbed back up to the kitchen and

padded into the sitting room. There was a red phone on a table beneath the back window. I called the motel and asked for Mrs Bergman by the name she'd registered under. After a while they put me through.

'Thanks for the call,' she said.

I could hear falsetto chattering punctuated by bursts of inane laughter. I guessed she was watching the television set in her room.

'Any problems?' I asked.

'I'm lonely, bored and scared,' she said, in her weak-little-woman voice. 'Apart from that I'm perfectly fine. Have you any news for me?'

'Nothing definite. But I've a lead that seems promising.'

'Must I stay in this motel?' she said plaintively. 'The food's synthetic and I'm bored to death watching television.'

'I think you should, Mrs Bergman. Less than twenty-four hours ago you just escaped being assaulted, remember? If they've not found what they're after they'll come looking for you. If they have they won't bother you again. Just try and give it a couple of days while we watch and see what happens.'

'I know you're right,' she said, and sighed down the line.

Neither of us spoke for a few moments. I listened to her breathing and the chatter from the television.

'Mr Lomax . . . ?'

I cleared my throat to let her know I was still there.

'I want you to know you can tell me anything you find out. I don't want you to keep anything from me.'

'Does that mean you're having second thoughts about your husband still being alive?' I asked.

'Certainly not,' she snapped. 'I . . . I was tired and upset last night when I said they may have killed him. They didn't find any book while I was there and, like you said, they'll need Carl until they find it because no one else knows where it is.'

Whether she was indulging in fantasies again or not, I decided she couldn't go on doing it for free any longer. So I said, 'Would it be possible for you to let me have an advance, Mrs Bergman? I have expenses and . . . '

'Of course, Mr Lomax,' she interrupted. 'You should have mentioned it sooner. Would a retainer to cover five days be acceptable?'

'That would be fine, Mrs Bergman.'

I was squirming inside. Asking for money is the lousy part of the business. Nine times out of ten you can see the suspicion shining from their eyes when you ask for an advance. Asking women is the worst. You don't like talking about money to the ones you find attractive and the ones you don't always let you know they think they're being ripped off. Trouble is, most of the time you're only bringing them bad news, and who likes paying through the nose for that?

'There's a post box here. I have your address. I'll mail you a cheque this evening.'

'I'd appreciate that, Mrs Bergman.' I'd have appreciated it more if she'd asked me to call at the motel and pick it up. All the same, I hoped she hadn't guessed how relieved I was.

'You'll call me if there are any developments?'

'I'll call you anyway,' I said. 'And whatever you do, don't leave the motel.'

She promised, and gave me a breathless goodbye before I cradled the receiver.

I began my search of the house by sifting through the jumble of files and papers strewn over the floor in Carl Bergman's study. Then I moved to the master bedroom where Estelle Bergman must have made a hurried attempt, early that morning, to gather up the clothes and tidy them away. I was pretty thorough. I checked the backs and undersides of drawers and furniture to see if anything had been taped there, looked behind radiators, checked for loose boards around the perimeter of the carpet. In the bathroom I ran my hand behind the pedestals and the hot water cylinder in the airing cupboard. I climbed onto the landing balustrade and managed to keep my balance while I lifted the hatch into the roof space and groped around the rim of the hole.

I had to abandon the search before I'd finished. The rooms had become gloomy in the evening twilight and I didn't want to switch on the lights and let the neighbourhood know I was there. It had all been a waste of time. All I'd got out of it was a dry-cleaning bill, dirty hands, a split fingernail and a fist full of skinned knuckles.

★ ★ ★

There was hardly any traffic on the roads and the journey home from the Bergman's place took only a few minutes. The evening had that soft, velvety quality that often comes at the end of hot, August days.

I let myself into the bungalow. My sweat-soaked clothes felt cold against my skin now. I poured myself a whisky, added a splash of American dry and went into the kitchen. I found a couple of slices of bread at the back of the bin that weren't too stale and put myself a sandwich together. I took it into the bathroom and ate while I bathed, the whisky blurring the senses, fooling my taste buds enough for me to get the sandwich down.

I rooted out my only dark suit. It was

crumpled and stained. I sponged off what marks I could and by the time I'd brushed and pressed it, it might just have got by on an Oxfam Shop bargain counter. All dressed up and ready to go, I gave my tie a final tweak as I passed the hall mirror. In that suit and shattered after a sleepless night and a long, hot day, I looked like the before-man in a laxative ad'. It was the best I could do. With a little luck the Wetherton Country Club would be one of those soft lights and sweet music places. Anything brighter than candlelight and the suit would get me bounced out.

9

The Wetherton Country Club was isolated, well off the beaten track. Maybe they liked it that way to keep out rowdies and the lower orders. A coach load of trippers would pass the place maybe once in a million years, and only then if the driver was blind drunk and lost.

A stone manor house had been converted into the club. There was only a faded, unlit sign at the entrance to a tree lined drive to say it was there. A couple of acres of gravel covered car park surrounded the building, and the place was enclosed by massive chestnut trees. Moths swooped and dived in the beams of floodlights set to illuminate the mellowed stone.

The car park was crowded, but I managed to find a vacant slot beneath the trees and backed the Rover in. I climbed out and locked up. The building with its moat of gravel was like an island of light in a dark ocean of trees and undergrowth. Out there, away from the town, the scent of grass and earth and trees was heavy on the warm night air.

I did a circuit of the place, the gravel crunching under my feet. Apart from the occasional flicker when the entrance doors opened and shut, no lights showed. There were a couple of fire escape doors, secured on the inside, and round the back dustbins, metal barrels and bottle crates were stacked alongside what was probably the kitchen door.

I returned to the entrance and stepped through into the lobby. Some arty interior designer had given it the nineteen-twenties art deco treatment. Lamps, wallpaper, carpet and drapes; silver, powder blue and russet brown, all skilfully contributing to the effect. The lighting was soft, but not as soft as I'd have liked. I trod over the carpet towards a mahogany reception desk. Behind it a young woman fleshed out just beyond the point of plumpness was answering the phone. She cradled the receiver and glanced up at me. Brown eyes, a tiny nose and a Cupid's-bow mouth: she had a face like an angel. Plump women often do.

'Do you admit non-members?' I worked hard at a smile.

'Non-members usually come as the guests of members.' Her voice was clear and refined.

'I'm down from the Shetlands for a few days. Staying at the Royal in Barfield. The manager there recommended your club. I've been driving round for an hour in the dark trying to find the place.'

She pursed her lips and looked thoughtful. Her deep chestnut hair was gathered up on top of her head and I could see her ears. They were small, far too small to support the jet earrings that dangled below the lace collar of the cream silk blouse.

I tried even harder with the smile.

'Perhaps you could give me some evidence of your identity, Mr . . . ?'

I didn't give her a name. I pulled out my wallet and took from it a card an oil executive had given me the previous year when I'd been retained by the company. I glanced at the card to make sure I knew who I was, then handed it over.

'MacShane,' I said. 'Alan MacShane, I'm a legal executive for Tomasco Oil.'

She stared at the card, then passed it back to me. She was giving me a radiant smile now. I could see her teeth: delicate and tiny, they were like her hands and ears.

'That's fine sir,' she said. 'I hope you'll forgive me for being cautious, but the management are determined to keep the club select, and you'd be surprised how difficult that is these days. I'll get the visitors' book and sign you in.' Her manner had become warmer, more deferential.

She turned and reached up to a shelf at the back of the reception area. She had the kind of ample posterior that would have delighted Rubens. She returned with a leather bound book, opened it out, flicked through to the first blank page and began to enter the day and date in the appropriate spaces. Her brassiere could only have been designed by a suspension bridge engineer. He'd done a great job, supporting nature's generous endowment. She looked up, handed me the pen, then spun the book round. From the smile she gave me I could tell she knew he'd done a great job, too. It was the kind of smile that's as old as Eve.

I almost had to get the card out again to see who I was. Somehow I remembered the name I'd given and scribbled it on the sheet. I entered a phony oil rig as the address. I figured there was just a chance she'd think legal executives slept in their suits on the rigs.

'That will be twenty pounds, sir,' she said.

I fought hard to stop my smile turning into an inane leer with the shock. I gave the wallet another airing, pulled out five fivers and laid them on top of the book. I had a feeling even that might look stingy for an oil executive.

'Thanks,' I said. 'You've been most helpful.'

She nodded towards a pair of doors. 'Through there, sir. The bar is on your left and the cabaret is due to start in a few minutes.'

I pushed my way through the swing doors into a place where the air was warm and moist and the lighting low. They'd kept up the art deco treatment, but the walls and ceiling had been painted a dingy brown to emphasise the brightness of the lighting on stage. I sauntered round to the bar and climbed onto a stool. The barman was wearing a scarlet jacket and black bow tie. His hair had been blow waved. When he asked what he could get me he was struggling to keep a Yorkshire accent out of his lisping, high pitched voice. I figured he wouldn't give the female staff any trouble. I told him a neat whisky; I'd a pretty good idea I'd need it full strength to help me get over the price. I was right.

I was up on a walkway that swept in a great curve around the back of the place. I half turned from the bar and took in the scene. Before me was a series of shallow terraces that dropped down to a miniature dance floor. On the far side of the dance floor about a dozen musicians were grouped beneath a circular stage. Brightly lit silver curtains concealed whatever lay beyond that. On the terraces, seating curved behind the tables: arranged that way parties up to a dozen strong could dine together and all see the show. Lamps with petal shades cast a soft glow over the tables. Scarlet jacketed waiters were clearing away the remains of meals and getting stoop shouldered humping big trays of drinks around. The aroma of grilled meat and tobacco smoke was strong. I began to salivate. I'd not bothered to eat properly that day, and the club dustbins probably held more appetising things than the sandwich I'd put together earlier.

I threw back the whisky and asked for another. I slid a note across the counter. The barman handed me some change then went on polishing the glasses.

'I'm told Roxy Morningstar's singing tonight,' I said.

He sucked in his cheeks, kissed the air, then gushed, 'Oh yes, sir. Later on though. There's a comedian on first. Dead common he is. Vulgar. Made some very cruel jokes at my expense, I don't mind telling you. I can't think why Mrs Cassanopolis tolerates it.' He teased a curl back into place then resumed polishing. 'But Roxy, she's something else. So vivacious. Really sweet. She's always absolutely super to me. And her dresses! Oh,' he waved a hand that was hinged at the wrist, 'they give me wings for a week. They really do. Wings for a week.'

I sipped whisky and surveyed the punters. Men with hard faces, worried faces, calculating faces, florid faces; chewing cigars, relaxing with wives and sons and daughters. Sales rep's with their synthetic bonhomie pursued clients. Attentive Romeos worked hard at the charm in pursuit of women who lapped it up, women who feigned disinterest. Single women, married women: who cares these days?

The band was competent: organist, base guitar, drummer, some brass. Couples on the dance floor faced one another and did physical jerks to the music. No touching. The decor may have been nineteen-twenties but not the dancing. A few would-be John Travoltas were doing their geriatric best, but a dance floor no bigger than a couple of pool tables imposes limitations. There was some enthusiastic clapping when the music stopped and the dancers threaded their way back to the tables.

I turned back to the barman. 'Is Roxy Morningstar her real name?'

He kissed the air some more, shook his head emphatically, then leant over the bar and said in a hoarse stage whisper, 'Betty Fullbright. Barfield born and bred. She used to live near us when I was a kid and she still lives just outside town. I always call her Roxy, though, cos she doesn't like her real name spread around. And she's been super to me. She's going places, our Roxy.' He sighed. He seemed to want to get the dresses on and go places too. He held a glass up to the light, squinted at it, then resumed the polishing.

The lights went even lower. The band struck up an introductory number and a young comic bounced onto the stage. He began to work some very blue material: cheeky, fast delivery stuff with no pretence at sophistication. The older women in the audience lapped it up, screeching and rolling around. Husbands chewed cigars and looked embarrassed at the way their wives weren't even trying to hold back the laughter at things ladies shouldn't admit to knowing about. Maybe I hadn't been too wide of the mark when I'd said it was the brotherhood of wealth that bound the clientele together.

The comic gave an extravagant build up for Roxy Morningstar then faded from the stage. She swept out from behind the curtains holding a hand mike and belted out the first number; it was an energetic performance by a tall, raunchy blonde in a flame coloured, sequinned dress split up to the top of her thigh. The barman watched enraptured. The dress must have made him drool. But he couldn't have filled it: hormone treatment and plastic surgery wouldn't have given him a shape like Morningstar's. And the way she was bouncing around like a jelly on springs said it all belonged to her. She introduced the songs in a husky, breathless voice, then cavorted around the stage, gyrating to the music while she sang. The amplifiers were being driven hard. Even with three double whiskies blunting my senses the sound came slicing through the pain barrier most of the time.

She disappeared behind the silver curtain and the applause finally died. I tapped my glass on the polished wood and snapped the barman out of his trance.

'How can I get a message to Miss Morningstar?'

He eyed me with a sudden wariness, like a mother hen guarding a chick. 'Message? Message for Roxy?'

I nodded. 'There's a guy with me on the rig. Tony Maxwell. He asked me to look her up and give her a message. In person.'

I got out the legal executive's card and slid it across the bar. He frowned at it, chewing his lip.

'Oil man. Mm.' He sucked his cheeks in and patted the curls. 'Well, I'll try for you, but I get quite a few requests like this and Roxy always says no.'

'Tell her the message is from Tony Maxwell,' I urged. I figured Carl Bergman would be known to her by the name he'd used at the disco where they'd met.

He strutted over to a wall phone, dialled, and started talking in a low voice. All the time he was giving me the kind of looks public health inspectors save for festering pork pies.

He cradled the phone and strutted back. He leant over the bar and pointed towards a door at the end of the curved walkway. 'Go through there, sir. Down the steps and turn right. Roxy's dressing room is at the end of the corridor.' His voice was peevish. I guess he didn't want to share the meagre ration of attention she'd given him with anyone.

I thanked him, trod along the carpet and went through the door into a corridor that was about six feet wide. White glazed brick walls, concrete floor and naked forty watt bulbs contrasted with the luxury on the other side of the door. Sounds echoed as I went down the steps. It was cool through here. The smell of cooking and toilets overlaid an odour of ancient dust. I turned right, just like the man said, into a corridor maybe ten yards long.

A door crashed open and a thick arm

reached out and dragged me in. The two men were tall, at least six-six, stable door wide and heavy as dray horses. They wore tuxedos. One sported a short black beard and a sagging beer gut. The other close cropped sandy hair and a fancy shirt; he looked about forty pounds more athletic than the one with the beard.

'So you're the guy that's pestering Miss Morningstar.'

'Nobody's pestering,' I snarled.

I watched and said nothing. They possessed that relaxed arrogance that emanates from physically huge men. But theirs was more than arrogance, it was the brutish aura of men with an animal capacity for violence. They'd dragged me through a smoke-stop door into a lobby at the foot of some stairs that rose to an upper floor.

'What's your business with her?' Blackbeard asked that.

'I've got a message for her. I had her phoned and I was invited through.'

'That's what they all say,' sneered Sandyhair.

'Gervaise told Mr Percival you'd

mentioned a guy called Maxwell,' growled the one with the beard.

'What's that to you?' I grated.

My eyes moved warily from one to the other. Their eyes weren't moving. They were locked on mine. Threatening.

'It's what it means to the manager that matters,' sneered the guy with sandy hair. He inclined his head towards the stairs. 'Get moving. Mr Percival hates being kept waiting.'

⋆ ⋆ ⋆

The office on the far side of the door was windowless. Brown carpet tiles covered the floor; fluorescent lights bathed everything in a cold, shadowless light. A couple of grey filing cabinets stood against the far wall. The other two doors were both closed. Silver framed black and white photographs of entertainers, some autographed, studded the faded, fly-blown wallpaper. The single visitor's chair had been placed in the middle of the room facing a dark oak partnership desk that had nothing on its glassy top except a black telephone and a silver salver the size of a dustbin lid.

The bulging mountain of creamy-pink flesh behind the desk was busy pushing a napkin under heavy jowls. Pink, sausage-like fingers were struggling to tuck it into a tight collar. He nodded towards the visitor's chair.

'Sit down, Mr McShane. How's the oil business?'

The two men who'd brought me into the room were standing close behind me now, one on either side of the chair. They were sniggering at something.

'So so,' I grunted.

'I do hope you don't mind if I continue eating, Mr McShane, but I generally feel the need for a light snack around midnight.' His voice was thin and breathless.

I shook my head, not that I figured it would have made any difference if I'd said I did mind. I looked over the parts of him that weren't hidden by the desk. His hair was so heavily oiled it looked like a cap of black patent leather; the central parting was a straight white line. A pink tongue flickered in and out of his mouth, and his wet lips glistened like red worms. Moist brown eyes hardly spared me a glance. They were fixed with trance-like greed on a French loaf as long as his forearm. He slit the loaf down the middle, trowelled in some pats of butter then, with deft movements, forked into it slices of cooked meat and bits of salad from the salver. He added a touch of this and a touch of that from some small jars, wielding the knife like an artist laying an impasto of colour on canvas. All the time little anticipatory belches erupted from the vast interior and set his purple jowls trembling. The tongue flickered incessantly, feeding saliva to the writhing, worm-like lips as if to lubricate them and get them ready to ease the meal on its way.

He folded the loaf shut. Holding it with both hands, he kept the slit uppermost to contain the oozing mixture and fed a surprisingly long length of it into his mouth. He chewed rapidly, eyes half closed, swallowed, then said, 'How well do you know Tony Maxwell, Mr McShane?' He belched delicately.

'Fairly well. We're both employed by Tomasco Oil.'

I heard a suppressed guffaw behind me.

The mountain of flesh called Percival stopped chewing, swallowed his second bite, then said, 'Really Mr McShane, by Tomasco Oil. How fascinating. And how well does Mr Maxwell know Miss Morningstar?' Another length of the loaf disappeared and the rapid chewing started up again.

I shrugged. 'I guess he met her whilst he was on shore leave from the rig. I've no idea how well he knows her.'

I'd a pretty good idea by now he was spinning me along. He swallowed, pushed some more of the loaf into his mouth and got the jaws working.

'Dare I ask what was the nature of the message you were bearing to Miss Morningstar? It's not too personal, I trust.'

'He just asked me to give her his regards, say he was looking forward to seeing her on his next spell off duty.'

The lies weren't even sounding convincing to me now. The guys behind me were laughing out loud.

Percival consumed the last morsel of bread, tugged the napkin loose from his collar, wiped fat fingers, dabbed greasy lips. He gave a smug, replete little belch, then said, 'I think we should bring this silliness to an end, Mr Lomax. I know perfectly well who you are. I'm also well aware that Maxwell never saw an oil rig in his life, let alone worked on one. What I can't understand is why you're pestering Miss Morningstar.'

'Nobody's pestering,' I repeated. 'I asked and she said she'd see me.'

'You really are naive, Mr Lomax. I told the barman to send you through. Miss Morningstar has no idea you're here. If I allowed the female artistes to be pestered by every randy Tom, Dick and Harry they'd refuse to appear here. Now, I'll ask you again, why do you want to talk to Miss Morningstar?'

I didn't say anything. His moist brown eyes returned my stare: eyes that were now watchful and alert, not opaque with gluttony. I tried to figure out how I should handle the situation, but the gorillas in suits standing right behind me inhibited scheming. I decided to give him part of the truth and said, 'I've been hired by Maxwell's wife to find him. She's out of her mind with worry, desperate to get him back. I think he knew Miss Morningstar. I just wanted to talk to her, see if she'd any idea where he might be.'

The worm lips twisted into a smile. 'Maxwell married? You surprise me, Lomax. He certainly didn't act as if he was. I'm amazed any woman would want such a neglectful husband back. I've heard some man left his wife because of him. Maxwell's been living with her ever since, on and off.'

I shrugged. 'His personal life is none of my business. I've just been hired to find him.'

'Come now, Lomax, his behaviour was so flagrant no wife, no matter how stupid, could have failed to know of it. I just cannot believe the woman cares. Out of her mind with relief because he's gone, perhaps. Worry: never.'

I sat with my arms folded across my chest and stared back at him. I figured if

I'd given him the wrong-guy-in-the-coffin routine he'd have died laughing. I could hear the band playing a dance number; faintly, as if through a great many walls and doors. Louder than that was the slow, even breathing of the men standing behind me, and the impulses of a wall clock as its second hand jerked round. The smell of cooked meat, fresh and succulent, from the left-overs on the salver, reminded me again how little I'd eaten that day.

Purple jowls shivered as the man behind the desk cleared his throat. 'Come along, Mr Lomax, tell me why you really want to locate Tony Maxwell.'

'We've been through all that,' I growled.

'Really, Mr Lomax, I think it's reprehensible the way you're lying to me. I don't believe for a moment that any woman married to Maxwell would waste a penny trying to find him.'

'I've already told you,' I snapped. 'I don't know what the hell you want me to say.'

His eyes flicked up to meet the eyes of

the men behind me. He gave a little nod that set his jowls shaking; hands grabbed me and hauled me to my feet.

'If you insist on being obdurate and stupid I can't prevent you, Lomax. But you'd better stop pestering Miss Morningstar, and I suggest you tell Maxwell's wife what a dirty little philanderer her husband is. That way she'll be spared a lot of pain in the long run. Now my two friends are going to give you an idea what to expect if you don't do as you're told and stop making a nuisance of yourself.'

They began to frog march me back to the door at the top of the stairs.

'Not too rough, boys,' Percival called after us. 'Just a little appetiser.'

They half dragged me down the stairs, over the corridor and into some staff toilets. They shoved me across the floor towards a row of cracked wash-hand basins. I turned, wedged my back into the far corner of the room and watched them coming towards me. They advanced slowly, as if savouring the pleasure of roughing me up. I pressed myself tighter into the corner. I knew I had to stay on my feet. If I fell they'd kick me to death.

Rust stained urinals were ranged against the wall behind them, and flimsy partitions screened off a couple of porcelain thrones. The faint sounds of rattling crockery and whistling just penetrated a door on my right. The floor was wet, especially around the urinals, and there was a pungent odour that the disinfectant couldn't hide.

On a sudden, panicky impulse, I wrenched a soap dispenser from the wall beside me and flung it at the one with the beard. It just bounced off his shoulder, dropped to the floor and burst open, its slimy contents slicking out over the concrete.

Blackbeard lunged forward. I jerked my head over. A rock like fist grazed my cheek and smashed into the tiling. I saw his eyes narrow with pain. He drew his fist back for a second try: he wouldn't miss again. I slammed him hard below the ribs. It was a pile driver of a punch, but it hardly made him pause in his stride. He closed in. I got my hands on the wash basins, lifted my foot into his stomach and heaved. He staggered back. The green slime from the soap dispenser was an oily film over the wet floor. He began to slip. Arms flailing like windmills, he reeled into the sandy haired guy and together they crashed into the cubicles. The flimsy chipboard partitions splintered aside. I heard a sickening, floor shaking thud as Sandyhair's forehead smashed into the rim of a pan.

I had to move fast. The bearded guy was on his hands and knees, trying to slither to his feet. I skirted the slime on the floor, grabbed a splintered door jamb and smashed it into the back of his head. He groaned with pain, but still tried to rise. I repeated the treatment four, maybe five times. After that he gave up the struggle. His face slumped into the concrete. The back of his head looked like a blood soaked bird's nest.

I tossed aside the piece of wood, straightened my jacket and tie. I caught sight of a flushed, wild eyed individual in a cracked mirror above the wash basins. The flood of adrenalin that had sustained the violent, animal intensity of it all still distorted my features. I took a few deep breaths, forced myself to relax, tried to get the trembling under control.

The other door burst open and an unshaven guy in a chef's hat and striped cotton trousers came through. His eyes moved up from the bearded man mountain to me, then down again to the twenty stone adonis with his head jammed in the lavatory pan.

His face slackened with shock. He pointed at Blackbeard with a whisk he was holding. 'What's the matter with Steve?' he gasped. Then he turned to the guy with his head in the pan, 'And Joe . . .'

'Steve has a migraine and Joe's just freshening up,' I said.

I nodded at the door he'd come through. 'Can I get out that way?'

He gazed at me, slack jawed and dumb.

'Can I get out that way?' I snapped.

'Yeah, brings you out at the back,' he said hurriedly.

I went through a small lobby into a cluttered, greasy kitchen that didn't seem any cleaner than the toilets. I pulled open a door on the far side of the kitchen, stepped out and found myself amongst the dustbins and beer crates I'd seen earlier. I wouldn't be that lucky next time. Next time they'd tear me into little pieces.

I got behind the wheel, started the engine, switched the lights on full beam and careered across the gravel. I cut in front of a Mercedes that was closing on the exit, showered it with stones as I slewed out, then accelerated through the gears, hurtling down the night-black country lane towards Barfield.

10

When Estelle Bergman said she'd mail me a cheque she hadn't made it clear whether she'd send it to the office or my home address: both were listed on the card I'd given her. The mail arrives at the bungalow around eight. I kept the door into the hall open while I sat in the kitchen drinking coffee and trying to make up for my lack of calories the previous day.

Footsteps approached, the letter flap rattled, then footsteps receded. I padded into the hall and picked up that morning's offering. A fatuous tax assessment, a demand for water rates and a gas bill bigger than Count Von Zeppelin's. But no cheque from Mrs Bergman, or anyone else for that matter.

I didn't want to linger around the bungalow; I figured the club bouncers might come searching for me to level the score. I managed to get a new shirt out of its wrappings without giving myself too much acupuncture treatment, then dressed in the lightest suit I had.

The effeminate barman had said Roxy Morningstar still lived in Barfield. I got the local directory. There was no one listed under her stage name, but there were a couple of Fullbrights and only one had an E for Elizabeth. I noted down the address.

It was a little after eight-thirty. If she was running true to form Melody would have arrived at the office. I went into the hall and dialled her number. She answered immediately.

'Could you unlock the box behind my mail slot and check the post for me?' I asked.

'Aren't you coming in, Paul?'

'Not for a couple of hours. I've got to attend to something first.'

'I hope I don't have to take any more calls from creditors. Some of them are getting pretty offensive.'

'No one could handle it better than you,' I said.

'Flatterer. Hang on, I'll get the key and check your box.'

The phone rattled onto the desk and I waited. Through an open door, the sitting room bay window gave me a view down the cul-de-sac. The near identical bungalows were meaner and dowdier than packing cases. That morning, with summer foliage hiding rotting window frames and faded concrete tiles, bright sunlight was making them look almost like homes.

I heard the phone scrape along the desk, then Melody said, 'I've collected your mail. There's not much. Do you want me to open it all?'

I asked her to open it up and search for cheques.

The phone rattled down again. I listened to the tear and rustle of paper for a few seconds.

'No,' she said presently. 'No cheques. And no bills or final demands either.'

I thanked her, told her I'd be in before lunch and cradled the phone.

I considered calling Mrs Bergman and reminding her about the advance she'd promised, but decided to leave it until later in the day. I went into the bathroom, stepped on a chair and pulled open a door that gives access to the cold water tank near the ceiling. I groped around the back of the tank and pulled out the polythene bag that contains my emergency funds. The roll was getting slender: it wouldn't have choked a canary, never mind a donkey. I peeled off a hundred in twenties and stashed what was left behind the water tank again.

Seconds later I was cruising out through the estate with the early morning mist rising like a curtain on what promised to be another scorching day.

* * *

Ten minutes steady driving around the outer ring road brought me to Roxy Morningstar's place. She may not have made the big-time, but the late registered Triumph sports car parked on the driveway of the detached bungalow said she was managing to keep the wolf from the door. I swung the Rover off the road and parked it behind the Triumph where a tall hedge of cypresses screened it.

I headed down the drive and across the front of the bungalow to an entrance door set behind an archway. I punched the bell and waited. A stoop shouldered guy with white hair and clean blue overalls was gently working a hoe around the flower beds. He looked almost as old as I felt. Neatly shaved turf was being given the treatment by an automatic sprinkler; a rainbow was hanging in the cloud of sparkling droplets. The bungalow was built ranch style of rough-hewn local stone, and the low-pitched roof had a wide overhang that held me in its shadow.

I got no answer, so I punched the bell some more and knocked on the panelled door for good measure. The old gardener was giving me the once over. I was just lifting my fist to give the door another pounding when it swung open.

Up close she was tall, really tall for a woman. In the gold sandals she was wearing she was only an inch or two shorter than me. Her white blouse had blue birds embroidered on it just below the right shoulder. Mirrored sun glasses with thin gold frames hid her eyes, but the mass of fluffy blonde hair, the big soft lips and emphatic figure were instantly recognisable.

'Miss Morningstar?' The question was rhetorical.

'That's right.' Off stage she didn't bother with the mid-Atlantic accent. It was obvious we both came from the back streets of the same Yorkshire town.

I handed her a card. I couldn't tell what reading it was doing to her, the dark shades hid her eyes and robbed her face of expression.

'So?' she said, and handed the card back to me.

'I'd like to talk to you about Tony Maxwell,' I said. I thought her body stiffened as I said that.

She stared at me through mirrored glass for a while, then said, 'You'd better come in.'

She stood aside and I stepped past her into the hall. She closed the door and led me into a sitting room that ran through from front to back.

'Sit down, Mr Lomax,' she said huskily.

I lowered myself onto pale green dralon.

She strode over to an onyx topped table, opened an onyx box and said, 'Cigarette?'

I shook my head.

She pressed one between her lips, flicked a gold plated Ronson and sucked the flame into the tobacco. She handled the lighter and dragged at the cigarette in an aggressive, almost masculine way. She flopped down on the armchair facing mine, stretched out her long, tight blue trouser clad legs and turned the dark glasses on me.

'I understand you're acquainted with Tony Maxwell,' I began.

She didn't say anything, just exhaled smoke through her nose.

'Maxwell,' I prompted. 'Tony Maxwell.'

'What's it to you?'

'I've been hired by his wife to find him. He's not been home for almost a month.'

'What makes you think I should know anyone called Tony Maxwell, let alone where he is?'

'I understand you've been seen

together, plenty of times. People tell me you were more than good friends.'

The big soft lips tightened. 'People? What people?' she snapped.

'That's my business,' I snapped back. 'I never reveal my sources, Miss Morningstar, just as I'll respect the confidence of anything you tell me. I'm just groping for a lead to Tony Maxwell, that's all. And I've got to find one fast. His wife's distracted.'

'Say, what is all this?' she pushed herself upright in the chair. 'I'll bet you're just raking through the dirt for some lousy divorce shake-down.' The Yorkshire accent was pronounced.

'Who said anything about divorce? I'm just trying to locate a missing husband.'

'Oh yeah. Well I think you're just some dirty little keyhole peeper poking his snotty nose into other people's business.'

'Listen, Miss Morningstar, I don't care what you do in public or private, or who you do it with. I'm just trying to find a missing husband.'

'You might not care, but my manager does. Things are really starting to happen for me career-wise, and I don't want involving in any divorce hassle.'

'I give you my word you won't be involved in any kind of hassle, divorce or otherwise. I'm just trying to find the guy.'

She took a long, slow pull at the cigarette and let the smoke trickle from her nose. Not being able to see her eyes was disconcerting. I couldn't gauge what she was thinking or feeling. She just sat there, not saying anything.

'Like I told you, his wife's distracted. And there's the kids, they're missing him. The medical company he works for want to contact him. If I don't reach him quick he won't have a job to come back to.' I hoped Carl Bergman had shot her the same line as the one he'd given the girl in the council flat when I said that.

'Kids,' she sneered. 'He didn't tell me about any kids. You're trying to con me. You must think I'm stupid. I wouldn't last a day in the entertainment business if I believed the stupid things guys like you tell me. You're just some perverted little keyhole peeper digging up the dirt so his la-de-da wife can get a divorce. Give you a thrill, does it, prying into other people's sex lives?'

'The lady doesn't have divorce in mind, Miss Morningstar. She knows nothing about her husband's extra-marital affairs. She just wants him back.'

She threw back her head and laughed. 'Extra-marital affairs,' she mimicked. 'I've heard it called a lot of things but that takes the prize. Look, Lomax, or whatever your name is, you can go and peer up your own keyhole. The only reason why you could be here is she wants a divorce. Company director: she'll take him to the cleaners.'

'Director?' I realised then that Carl Bergman made subtle changes in his spiel to suit the female he was pulling.

'Yeah. Synarcot, or something like that. She'd screw stacks out of him in a divorce settlement. So don't try and kid me you're just looking for the guy. I'm not stupid.'

'Maybe not,' I said gently. 'But you're stupid enough to shoot yourself full of dope.'

She went very still, and her mouth

compressed into a tight, hard line. She got up and moved, cat-like, to the onyx table; ground her cigarette into an ash tray, took another from the box and lit it with the gold Ronson. She turned and faced me, the cigarette wedged well down between her fingers, her elbow cupped in her other hand.

'I don't know what your game is,' she said coldly. 'But I think I'd like you to leave. Now, Mr Lomax.'

I grinned up at her insolently. 'I don't think so, Miss Morningstar. We'll finish our talk first.'

'It's finished, stupid,' she snapped. 'Now get out before I call the police.'

'I don't think you will call the police,' I said. 'Not with all the dope you've got stashed away here.'

'You're a nut case,' she croaked. 'A ruddy nut case. I've never used the stuff. I wouldn't dream of it, not in my position. In the public eye. I couldn't afford to.'

I recalled her performance the previous night; the limitless energy she'd had. The woman standing in front of me now was a shadow of the creature who'd strutted and pranced around the stage for upwards of an hour.

'I think maybe you can't afford to do without it,' I said gently. 'If you didn't have a shot before you went on stage you'd never work up a big enough head of steam to get through the act.'

'I'm telling you, I never touch the lousy stuff. So stop pestering me and clear out or I'll call the police.'

'You won't have to call the police. I'll call them if you don't start talking about Tony Maxwell. Just tell me what you know and I'll leave you in peace.'

'What does it take to get a message through your thick skull, Lomax.' Her voice was hoarse. She was almost screaming at me now. 'Get out of my house. Scram. Clear off.' She gestured with her thumb towards the door.

I guessed I'd reached the end of the line. She was a big girl in a tough business and she wasn't going to break under a little pressure. But I knew I wouldn't get another lead like this. I couldn't let it crash to a full stop in a brick wall called Morningstar.

'Give me what you know about Maxwell,' I urged. 'Then I'll clear out. If you don't I'll put a call through to the police, tell them you're on horse and snow.'

'You don't even know what the words mean,' she sneered.

I struggled to remember what the girl in the council flat had told me. 'Heroin and cocaine,' I said. 'Speedball. The drug cocktail that gives you a long enough buzz to get through the act.'

'Naff orf,' she yelled. She was breathing audibly through her open mouth and I could see big teeth that were too white and too perfect: the sort of mouth entertainers get after a lot of expensive dental work.

I rose slowly to my feet and sauntered over thick, cream coloured shag pile carpet. I lifted the handset of a phone that was standing in an ornamental plaster niche and began to dial.

'Who the hell do you think you are?' she snarled. 'And what the hell do you think you're doing?'

I turned and gave her a bored little

smile. 'Dialling the police,' I said. 'I'll see if I can get them to send the drug squad over with a dog to sniff around the place and a doctor to take a look at the jab marks on your arms.'

Something seemed to snap inside her. She leapt at me like a frenzied animal, began to slap my face: heavy, open handed blows. She was no featherweight and I'd be lying if I said it didn't hurt. She shaped her hands into claws, reached up and sank painted nails into the crown of my scalp. Her mouth was slack. I could feel her tobacco tainted breath moist and hot in my face. She began to draw her hands towards my temples. I could feel her nails ripping through my scalp. I dropped the phone, grabbed her wrists and managed to pull her hands away before she could scratch me where it showed. I squeezed her wrists tighter. She squealed and went limp. She was panting with exertion.

'Pig,' she said. 'You filthy rotten pig.' She literally spat the words into my face; I could feel beads of her saliva on my cheeks.

I forced her back into her chair, let go of one of her wrists and tore the sunglasses from her face. Big eyes glared hate at me. They were the palest grey, like a winter sky reflected on ice. The whites were bloodshot. I pulled her arm out straight, pushed up the sleeve of her blouse. The scabby needle marks were there all right, and a flesh coloured dressing probably hid some that were new.

'Satisfied?' The husky, tearful voice was like another slap in the mouth.

'Maxwell,' I growled. 'Tell me everything you know about Maxwell, or I'm phoning the police.' I let her arm drop, stepped back and sat in my chair.

'Like what?' she asked.

'Like when you last saw him, for starters.' I said.

She closed her eyes. Her trembling lips shaped unspoken words as if she were working something out. 'Three weeks ago, as of yesterday,' she said presently. 'I can remember it because he brought me home from the Club. Mostly he used to let himself in with his key and wait for me.'

'Go on,' I urged.

'Go on what?'

'Talking about Maxwell. So far you've said nothing.'

She shrugged. 'He generally stayed 'til about three, then he left for his hotel. He didn't want to cause gossip for me. The nosy parkers around here have tongues a yard long.'

'When did you meet him?'

'Say, what is all this? I thought you just wanted to find him,' she said angrily.

'I'll ask the questions,' I said. 'When did you meet him?'

'Oh, maybe six months ago. My manager booked me a gig at a disco. He thinks I should widen my appeal. Tony was there. He was the only mature, decent looking guy in the place. Something just clicked: you know how it is. He was gentle and sensitive and sensual with it. He was just ... wonderful.' She'd gone all starry-eyed at the memory. She suddenly snapped out of it, scowled at me, and added, 'Not like you, you great

141

thick pig.' She rubbed her wrists. 'You've hurt me.'

'You weren't exactly tickling me,' I said wryly.

'Pig,' she snarled.

'So we've had the hearts and flowers stuff,' I said, ignoring the invective. 'What about the other things he was doing for you?'

'I don't know what you mean.'

'Giving you what you need most,' I said. 'The horse and snow to keep you coping. I always thought applause is the thing entertainers crave. Seems I was wrong.'

'How would you know, you dirty little keyhole peeper. Don't you have a life of your own to lead instead of sticking your nose into my business. Give you a thrill, does it, digging up the dirt? You snotty little pervert.'

'Just answer the questions, or I'll put that call through to the police.'

'What if he did give me the occasional shot?' she said petulantly. 'I'm not a kid anymore. I can handle it. And he'd got access to stacks. Judas Priest, his lousy firm processes the stuff.'

'But he gave you more than the occasional shot, didn't he? He gave you all you wanted.'

She shrugged. It was a final acknowledgement of defeat. 'Okay, okay. So he gave me plenty. But I was doing plenty for him, too. We were great together.'

'He didn't take drugs himself?'

'No. He was very placid. A relaxed kind of guy, not the type to have the need.'

'Did he ever talk to you about the drugs scene, the way it all works?'

She gave me a foxy look. 'Are you sure you're private? I don't see what all this has to do with finding him.'

'I'm not from the police,' I said. 'What you do is no concern of mine. But if you don't make with the answers I'll get the cops in.'

'We did talk about the drugs scene. We talked about it a lot. What else? But he wasn't like some nark from the Truth and Light Brigade. He didn't judge. He understood and accepted me as I am.'

'And where do you think he is now?' I asked.

'I don't know,' she said. 'I wish I did.' Her voice was husky and tearful and her lips were trembling. 'Like I told you, three weeks as of yesterday was the last time I saw him. We had an almighty row. He used to leave a few clothes here. I found a letter in a jacket, from some woman in Ramford City. An educated bitch, you could tell that from the letter. She'd got the hots for him and she was writing about it in a way I could hardly understand. I wasn't being two-timed by some clever little tart. So, like I said, we had this row and I've not seen him since.'

She buried her head in her hands and began to weep quietly. 'And I miss him. I've never met anyone like him. I miss him like hell. I wish I'd never found the lousy letter.' She spoke the words softly, more to herself than to me, in the husky singer's voice that was rough and throaty with crying.

'Have you still got the letter?'

She shook her head but didn't look up. The fluffy, bottle blonde hair was all around her face and shoulders.

'Can you remember the address?'

'No,' she sobbed and shook her head some more.

'What about the clothes he left? Have you still got those?'

She raised her blotchy, tear stained face. 'I burnt the damn things. I couldn't bear the sight of them every time I opened the wardrobe door.'

'So you've absolutely no idea who the woman was or where she lives?'

'All I know is she's some clever, over-educated little bitch from Ramford who calls herself Sheba,' she bawled tearfully.

I eyed her steadily for a few seconds, then worked my lips into a smile.

'You callous pig,' she sobbed venomously. 'You just don't care. You've got what you wanted. You've got me into this state, and now you're going to clear off.'

'I'll clear off,' I said, 'when you've told me one more thing. Who's supplying you with drugs now lover boy's gone?'

'There's plenty around,' she said evasively. 'I do okay.'

'Not the kind of stuff you're using. Who's feeding you. Just tell me that and I'll go and leave you in peace.'

'You don't understand these things,' she moaned. 'They'd stop supplying me if it got around that I'd been talking. I could even get hurt.'

'It's not going to get around. All I want are the facts, the full picture. So I can get some idea where Tony Maxwell might be.'

She lifted her eyes to mine. 'Okay,' she said. 'I'll tell you. But she'll send her boys and they'll kill me if she ever finds out I've split. I get a supply from Mrs Cassanopolis. She gives me all I want. No problems.'

'Mrs who?'

'Cassanopolis. She owns the Wetherton Country Club.'

Something fretted away at the corners of my mind. Then I remembered the barman at the club had mentioned the name.

I rose to my feet. 'Thanks Miss Morningstar. Don't worry about having told me the things you have. All I'm trying to do is find Tony Maxwell for his wife. She won't find out about your involvement with him from me, and the drugs thing is none of my business.'

'If you find him, tell him I didn't mean the things I said. Tell him . . . Tell him I need him bad.'

I gazed down at her. Tousled blonde hair, tear-stained face; without the stage make-up, the bright lights, most of all without the dose of heroin and cocaine, she looked jaded, used, older than her years. Her sun glasses lay smashed where we'd trampled them into the carpet, and her dropped cigarette had burnt a neat black hole in the dralon.

'I'll see myself out.'

'You can see your ugly backside in the hall mirror for all I care,' she said.

I stepped through the front door. The old gardener was working away steadily with the hoe and the sprinkler was still keeping the turf fresh. I climbed into the Rover. The seat was hot against my back.

While I waited for a break in the traffic I reflected on the stroke I'd just had to pull to earn the lousy money Mrs Bergman hadn't even bothered to pay me: brawling with some drug-crazy woman who needed all the psychiatric help she could get.

I saw a gap in the stream of cars. I let out the clutch and left a lot of rubber at the end of Morningstar's drive as I accelerated onto the ring road and headed back into town.

11

I got behind the desk in my attic office, put my feet up and tried to piece together the information I'd harvested over the past forty-eight hours. I realised now why Estelle Bergman hadn't wanted the police in. She'd got it right when she'd said her husband researched material for his articles in unorthodox ways. But she couldn't have known of his involvement with other women, not the way she was still carrying a torch for him.

Through the open window I could hear the steady rumble of down-town traffic and, closer at hand, the phutt-phuttering of mowers struggling with the long grass in the church yard opposite. A tired breeze wafted in humid air that was gritty with dust and spiced with the smell of freshly cut grass. I caught the faint whirring sound of old machinery getting ready for action, then the church clock began to chime. I counted twelve.

The clanging of the bell was so loud through the open window it had masked the sound of footsteps and opening doors. I didn't realise someone was with me until I felt the papers on the desk being shoved around. I opened both eyes.

'Sleeping on the job again, are we?' Melody chirped brightly. She finished clearing a space for the tray and laid it down on the desk.

'Thinking,' I said sternly, 'not sleeping. That's what separates the men from the boys in this business. And, may I add, makes all the difference between your job and my vocation.'

I dragged my feet off the desk and inspected the tray.

She gave me an indignant look, then decided to laugh. 'Cheeky,' she said. 'You're getting quite out of hand these days.'

I grinned up at her. 'Like to try and tame me?'

She giggled. A blush that was barely noticeable beneath the summer tan touched her cheeks, and I knew she'd deliberately steered the conversation into safer waters when she said, 'I sent Moira to the delicatessen for sandwiches and asked her to bring you some. Ham: is that okay?'

'Ham's just fine,' I said. 'How much do I owe you?'

'Oh, settle it later,' she murmured tactfully.

I looked up at her. Her white dress contrasted with the tan and the dazzling blonde hair fell into a mass of curls on her shoulders. Morningstar was blonde and glamorous in a stagey kind of way, but Melody was taking all the prizes. She seemed cool and fresh despite the humid, gritty heat. Perhaps it was what there was of the dress she was wearing, or perhaps it was the subtle messages her expensive perfume was sending. Either way, I must have been looking at her too intently for comfort because she began to colour up again.

I took a sip at the coffee and said, 'Any more trouble from creditors?'

She shook her head. 'Not since yesterday, I think they've given up for the time being. But it's the calm before the storm,' she warned, and I detected the concern in her voice.

She flicked at the far corner of the desk with a swatch of papers to clear the dust, then perched her shapely little posterior on the battered wood. 'Two men came up to see you this morning though,' she said.

I gulped down a mouthful of half chewed ham. 'Men?'

'Yes. They said they had a business appointment. I told them you were out but they insisted on coming up here to make sure. They seemed angry.

'What kind of men?'

'Tall. Awfully tall. Even taller than you. And big. One was so massive he looked grotesque. The other wasn't quite as bad.'

'The really big guy, did he have a black beard?'

'That's right. He wore a hat, too. Strange, really, in all this heat.'

I nodded, took another bite and chewed thoughtfully. The black bearded guy must have had a cast-iron skull to recover so quickly. He was probably wearing a cap to cover the bandages.

A worried look came into her eyes.

'They weren't a couple of bailiffs, were they?'

I smiled. 'I don't think so. I don't owe rates on the office, just on the bungalow.'

She gave a despairing sigh. 'You're the absolute limit, Paul.'

'Did they leave any message?'

'No. But like I said, they seemed angry when they left and they were so huge it was scarey. You really do seem to rub shoulders with some violent looking people.'

'Sometimes it's more than just rubbing shoulders.'

I ate the last of the sandwiches, drained the cup of coffee and relaxed back in the chair. Perched on the far corner of the desk, Melody was bathed in sunlight and sunlight suited her. The faint breeze that was wafting in through the window was just strong enough to move her hair.

She must have noticed that look coming back into my eyes because she slid off the desk and picked up the tray. 'Well,' she said, in a no-nonsense voice, 'if you don't have any work to do, I certainly have.' She turned and headed for the door. The white dress with the thin shoulder straps plunged even more dramatically at the back than it did at the front, and the gentle tan flowed in an unbroken tide all the way down.

★ ★ ★

The pavement was hot through the paper thin soles of my brogues as I trudged towards the market place and the car. Men in shirt sleeves, women in summer dresses: the hottest August for a decade, or so the weather men kept saying. Nearer the market place, litter and 'For Let' signs and harassed faces and dirty glass and flaking paint kept reminding me I was in Barfield, Yorkshire; not Bath on Avon.

I couldn't make up my mind what to waste my time on next. I'd not completed the search of the Bergman residence, although something told me I wouldn't find any notebook there, and I had to look over Roxy Morningstar's place; wait until she went out then check whether or not she really had thrown away Carl Bergman's clothes and the letter from the educated dame in Ramford City. I climbed inside the four-wheeled oven and figured I'd let the first break in the traffic decide which way I went and which job I tackled that afternoon.

The gap came. I turned towards the outer ring road and Roxy Morningstar's place.

On the way I stopped off at a phone booth and dialled the hotel where Mrs Bergman was staying. Correction: had been staying. A bored female said she'd left first thing that morning and driven off in a taxi. That worried me. She hadn't left any message for me or any phone number. Suddenly my not inconsiderable investment of time and effort seemed even less likely to result in a pay-out.

I motored slowly past the Morningstar bungalow. The Triumph sports car had gone from the drive, the sprinkler had stopped sprinkling and the gardener had finished his stint. I took the first left and parked the Rover down a road where large and exclusive bungalows were spaced out by lawns and trees.

I strolled down Morningstar's drive,

crossed the front of the bungalow and rang the bell. There was no answer. I got out the bunch of keys I'd salvaged from Carl Bergman's document case and began to try them in the lock. None fitted. Maybe Carl Bergman, or Tony Maxwell as he liked to be called when he went out on the town, discreetly kept those keys on a separate ring.

I headed round the bungalow. The back garden was more generous than back gardens usually are these days. Neat flower beds and a lawn with an ornamental pool were enclosed by a dense green pallisade of cypress trees. No one was lounging on the pink candy-striped sun bed. The place was deserted.

I found a shovel beside the dustbin, wedged it into the rebate of the kitchen window fanlight, and applied leverage while I pounded the frame. The fanlight was used a lot, the ones in kitchens generally are, and the metal on the peg and stay was shiny. The vibration soon shook the stay free and the fanlight flipped open. I reached inside, unfastened the larger window, then clambered over sill and sink unit and dropped into the kitchen.

White cupboard units, pale blue walls, pink terrazzo tile floor. The washer, spin dryer, cooker and fridge were enamelled a deep blue: all good quality new looking gear. I released the latch on the back door just in case I had to make a quick exit, then began with the cupboards and drawers. It didn't take long. Morningstar wasn't a hoarder. Some of the drawers were almost empty. I checked out cereals packets, food containers, the fridge; all the not-so-smart places people hide things when they think they're being cute. I found nothing. Not even a speck of dirt or a smear of grease or a crust to indicate she'd ever cooked a meal in there.

I moved on into the sitting room where I'd argued with her that morning. The broken sun glasses were in the ashtray on the onyx table and when I checked the sofa and armchairs I saw she'd turned the cushion of the chair to hide the cigarette burn. I worked my way through the cupboards and drawers in a hand-some mahogany sideboard. I found rate demands, gas bills, the usual papers people accumulate. In the central compartment, stashed amongst empty and nearly empty bottles of spirit, was a folder of fan mail, a box of glossy autographed photos of Morningstar bursting out of a black, sequinued dress and a swatch of duplicated reply letters. I did a rapid check through it all to make sure she'd not hidden other letters there. She hadn't, but a lot of the fan mail made lewd references to the more striking aspects of the Morningstar anatomy.

I moved across the hall into the front bedroom where some more of the cream shag pile carpet was brushing my ankles. A coverlet of what looked like wolf fur had been laid over black silk sheets on a water bed. I guess the tide was in: when I tried to give it the once over it heaved up and down like it was breathing. The walls were lined out with brown cork and the furniture was all varnished pine and brass handles.

I sorted through the contents of the wardrobe, the dressing table and the chest of drawers. By that time I'd been in the place almost an hour and I was getting pretty edgy. I found myself glancing more and more frequently through a stagey arrangement of net curtains that obscured the front window. Even so, I was thorough. There was no point risking a breaking and entry rap for a skimped search job. There were no letters and no men's clothes, just a syringe and a couple of blood smeared swabs wrapped up in a face towel and hidden beneath some clothes in one of the dressing table drawers.

I left the bedroom and tried the next door along the hall. It opened into a jade green bathroom where body sprays and bath oil and the like were lined up on a tiled window sill. There were no shelves or cupboards to search.

A shallow airing cupboard opened off the hall. I worked my hands beneath layers of wool and linen, searched behind the hot water cylinder, and found nothing.

The warmth inside Morningstar's hygienic odourless bungalow, and my own nervous tension, were making sweat ooze from my body. I padded back to the front bedroom window and checked the approaches. They were all clear.

I went into the back bedroom. Inexpensive blue carpet covered the floor and the walls were painted matt white. Cotton dust sheets protected two chromium plated racks of dresses: the kind of long racks dress shops use. They were the only things in the room. I flicked through the brightly coloured and sequinned gowns. There were no men's clothes lurking there and no hiding places for a letter. If Morningstar had kept any mementos of her passionate fling with Carl Bergman, alias Tony Maxwell, I certainly hadn't found them. I pulled the dust sheets back and began to take one last look round before I left the room.

I heard a key scraping in a lock, the sound of the front door opening and closing, a pleading woman's voice. I froze behind the nearest rack of dresses. Footsteps, muffled by carpet, thudded down the hall then clattered onto kitchen tiles. All the time Morningstar was coaxing, wheedling, begging a silent companion.

'What the hell have I done wrong? Just tell me,' she demanded tearfully.

'You've upset Mrs Cassanopolis, sweetie. And that's not sensible.' It was the man speaking.

'Look, all I want is the usual. And I've got to have it before I go on stage tonight.' Her Yorkshire accent, surfacing again under stress, was a harsh contrast with the man's calm, slightly affected refinement.

'You are a silly girl, getting yourself addicted like that.'

'I'm not addicted,' she yelled.

'You could have fooled me, sweetie.'

'Look,' she said, lowering her voice and trying to make it sound reasonable. 'Just for tonight. Before I go on. All I want is my usual delivery. You've no idea what it's like, going on stage cold. I've got to have it. I can't get through the act without it.'

'But we've been naughty, haven't we? Mrs Cassanopolis is quite upset.'

'Sod Mrs Cassanopolis,' she screamed. 'I've not seen her for a month. How the

161

hell can I have upset her when I don't even go near her?'

'Visitors. You've been having visitors, haven't you?'

'Visitors? What's that supposed to mean?'

'You know very well what it means. I'm talking about some of your male visitors.'

'Why the hell shouldn't I have men visitors? I'm not a nun. What's my private life got to do with that silly bitch?'

'No one, but no one, cares how many men beat a path to your front door, sweetie. Mrs Cassanopolis is just worried about your indiscretions with certain ones.'

'I don't know what you mean.' The cold, quiet voice said she did know what he meant, and she didn't like it.

'Tony Maxwell, for starters,' he said. 'You know what a rumpus he caused back at the ranch when you started pouring your heart out to him and he began poking his nose into things.'

'But I've had all that out with her. Mrs Cassanopolis believed me when I told her

I'd no idea what his game was,' she said plaintively.

'True, sweetie, but we've forgotten our lesson haven't we? We still can't keep our pretty little mouth shut.'

'I don't know what you're talking about. And what's all this we, we, sweetie crap. You patronising little berk. You sound like some limp-wristed old queen.'

'Just watch what you're saying, Roxy, or I'll make sure you never get so much as an aspirin out of Cassanopolis.' Anger had chased the mockery from his voice. 'I'm talking about the caller you had this morning: Lomax. The private investigator who's looking for Maxwell. What were you stupid enough to tell him?'

'Nothing,' she bawled tearfully. 'I couldn't have told him anything if I wanted to, cos I don't know where Tony's gone. Anyway,' she finished thoughtfully, 'how do you know he was here.'

'Your gardener, sweetie. You don't think Mrs Cassanopolis let you borrow one of hers from the club because she wanted to do you any favours, do you? He's been keeping an eye on the place since the

Maxwell business.'

I heard Morningstar mutter, 'The bitch,' then her tone became wheedling and seductive and she tried hard to work a little refinement back into her husky voice as she said, 'I don't know why you and me are arguing like this. I just don't. We've always got along so well.' Her voice became softer, huskier: 'And we could get along even better. I could be really good to you, Ron.'

'If you're offering what I think you're offering, sweetie, no thanks. Heavens knows, I'm no prude. But I like a woman to be a little more exclusive than a public convenience.'

I heard a loud slap followed by a thud and a rattle of crockery. I figured she'd smacked his head back into one of the cabinets.

'You cheap little tart,' he exploded angrily.

I caught the sound of blows and struggling.

'Don't mark me. Please don't mark me,' she squealed, 'I'm on stage tonight.'

While they were hard at it I shoved my

head around the bedroom door and glanced across the hall. The kitchen door was ajar. It suddenly crashed shut as they fell against it. Morningstar's line of abuse was a sight more original than it had been with me that morning. Judging by the yells the guy was giving out I figured she was busy with her nails again. I emerged from the bedroom, glided down the hall and stepped out through the front door.

I cut across the front of the bungalow and headed down the drive. Morningstar's Triumph TR7 wasn't so new looking any more. The front nearside wing was crumpled and a deep scratch ran the length of the car. Sun glasses, burnt cushion, an expensive bodywork job, an altercation with me in the morning and a brawl with a guy called Ron in the afternoon. It wasn't Roxy's day. And to cap it all she didn't seem to be having much success getting the shot of dope she needed to carry her through.

12

Cigarette smoke, a stranger lurking amongst familiar household smells, should have put me on my guard. But I was too hot and tired and eager to get my hands on a drink to read the sign. When I pushed through the sitting room door a fist like an iron ball smashed the breath out of me. I doubled up. Twin mountains of flesh closed in, forced me against the wall.

I wrapped my arms over my face and head and tensed myself against the hail of kicks and blows. Their revenge taking seemed to last a century. I reeled and crashed around amongst the furniture. They left my head and face alone, but the beating they gave the rest of my body was brutal and ruthless. I began to black out. I felt them dragging me into the kitchen, heard the crash and clatter of dishes and pans being swept aside, then felt the icy shock of water pouring onto the back of my head from the tap over the sink.

The red dark began to clear, sounds stopped echoing, I got my ragged breathing under control. They pulled me up from the tea leaves and clotted left overs of that week's meals. I slumped down on a kitchen stool.

'Sixteen stitches,' Blackbeard snarled. 'That's what I had to have after you worked me over.' The recollection revived his rage and he gave me another savage kick just below the knee.

I glared hate at him through a mist of pain.

The one with sandy hair was looking around the tiny kitchen. 'What a tip. We were going to smash the place up but it's such a dump you wouldn't know we'd tried.'

They sneered down at me for a while, then Blackbeard inclined his head towards the door and snapped, 'On your feet.'

I put my hands on the table, forced myself up, then shambled towards the front door.

'I'll come with you,' the sandy-haired guy said. 'Sid can follow in our motor. You drive.'

'Where to?'

'Wetherton Country Club. Cassanopolis wants a talk. Move it, Lomax. And no tricky driving or you'll get some more of the same.'

★ ★ ★

The sandy-haired minder was a silent, menacing presence. He didn't speak a word during the twenty-minute trip to Wetherton Country Club and I was too busy trying to cope with the pain that breathing and driving were causing me to ask any questions.

I turned into the gap in the foliage and motored on between tall trees. A couple of minutes later the wheels crunched over the gravel parking area and stones peppered the underside of the car. I rolled to a stop near the entrance. The tail car pulled up alongside.

They led me into the club, took me through a door behind the reception desk, then held my arms while we made our way up a wide flight of stairs. The interior seemed pitch black after the brilliant sunlight. Windows were shuttered or curtained over with heavy velvet drapes, and the only illumination came from dim safety lights. The place had that stale, dusty smell that always invades the silent spaces left in clubs and theatres after the crowds have gone.

We reached a wide landing that curved into the darkness. The void beyond the balusters to my left was a black emptiness, and the delayed echo of our feet thudding on carpet gave me a feeling it was cathedral size. Some of the doors on my right were open. In the feeble glow of isolated safety lights I could make out roulette wheels and gaming tables.

When we got to the end of the landing the sandy-haired guy opened a door and Blackbeard grabbed my arm and steered me through. In the near dark I tripped and fell onto another flight of stairs. They dragged me upright, and I followed Sandyhair up into the blackness. He pushed a door open at the top and we stepped into a shaft of sunlight that was burning its way through a dirt streaked dormer window. I screwed my eyes shut against the sudden brightness. When I opened them again I saw we were at the end of a long gallery that must have been located just beneath the apex of the roof. Flakes of old whitewash were hanging amongst the cobwebs that festooned the vaulted, plaster ceiling. At the far end, another dormer window was letting some more light filter in.

We trod over uneven boards that had been swept clean, then stopped about half-way down the gallery where a heavy timber door was hidden away at the end of a short cross vault. A louvred plastic box was fixed to the wall beside the door.

The guy with sandy hair shoved his face up to the box, pressed a switch at the side, and said, 'Orville and Miller here, with Lomax.'

He released the switch and a thin, metallic voice said, 'Bring him up.'

The thud of electrically operated bolts set the door vibrating. Blackbeard grabbed a metal handle and pulled it open. Sandy-hair went through first, Blackbeard pushed me after him, then tagged along behind. We trudged up the narrow, spiral staircase in single file. I didn't count the steps, but at a guess I'd say we climbed up another twenty feet or so before we passed through a doorway into an octagonal room about fifteen feet across. Seven of the facets contained a small, arched window; the eighth held the door we'd entered through.

A round oriental carpet covered most of the oak boarded floor. At its centre was an oak refectory table. Behind the table was an oak chair with a high, richly carved back.

A diminutive, doll-like woman of indeterminate age sat in the chair. Deep set eyes, like tiny beads of black glass, gleamed out of a round, swarthy face. Her nose was flat and small, and the ends of her lipless mouth turned down into the rootlike network of wrinkles that fissured the weathered skin. An abundance of wiry, iron grey hair was massed around her head. She wore a black crepe-de-chine dress fastened right up to the neck with black cloth covered buttons. The sleeves were full and gathered at the wrists by tight cuffs. Her tiny, wrinkled fingers were laced together. They rested on the table, and her hands and forearms were reflected sharply in its polished top. Her only jewellery was a plain wedding ring. Her fingernails were white against the dark, mottled flesh of her hands. They'd been cut short and carefully manicured. She wouldn't have reached the finals in a glamorous grandmother competition, but she'd have made a great bride for one of Snow White's seven dwarfs.

I stood in front of the table, the two giant minders right behind me. The beating they'd given me back at the bungalow had left me in bad shape and I was gasping after the climb into the stratosphere.

'You seem to be rather out of condition, Mr Lomax, which is all the more reason why I should thank you for coming up here to see me.' The clear, strong voice that came from the tiny body surprised me. She had a heavy Greek accent.

'I think perhaps that you should sit down.' She nodded towards a stool. The stool and a brass telescope mounted on a tripod were the only other objects in the room. I lowered myself gratefully onto its leather top.

'How do you like my little eyrie? I think I have your English word correct: the abode of eagles. I find high, isolated places spiritually uplifting. Do you not find them so, Mr Lomax? During the ascent one seems to be shedding one's sullied, earth-bound self to emerge a pure, free spirit at the summit. I am sure that is why the religious of my own country perch their monasteries like eagles' nests in high mountain places, for it is only there that the spirit can soar free.'

I thought I'd got the drift of what she was trying to tell me. At least it explained why I always got a touch of the old black dog if I lingered in my stunted little bungalow much after nine in the morning.

She must have noticed the glazed look in my eyes and decided she was casting her pearls before a particularly stupid swine because she said, 'Forgive me, Mr Lomax, I appear to be trying your patience and that is the last thing I must do after you have been so kind as to come and talk with me.'

She raised her eyes to the men behind me. 'You may leave us now. Wait beside the lower door until I call.'

I heard them crossing the boards, then shoes scraping on stone as they descended the steps. Two windows, on opposite sides of the tower, were open. At that height the breeze wafting through felt cool on my skin. Over the tops of the forest trees that enclosed the place I could see golden fields shimmering in the heat.

She cleared her throat to regain my attention. I turned my aching head towards her. Coal black eyes glittered at me from deep within folds of sallow, wrinkled flesh.

'I understand you are trying to locate a man who calls himself Tony Maxwell?'

I nodded. 'Your manager, the guy called Percival, went over the same ground with me last night, Mrs Cassanopolis. I told him all I know.'

'But you decided not to heed his warning.'

I raised an eyebrow.

'To stop your search for the man and above all to stop pestering the girls who perform at my club.'

'If I stopped probing every time I touched a raw nerve I'd get nowhere in this job,' I said.

'Your expression, raw nerve, is most apt. Tony Maxwell touched many raw nerves. May I ask if you are having any success with your search for the man?'

'None,' I said. 'The only lead I was following hasn't taken me anywhere. I think I'm going to call it a day and tell my client I can't trace her husband.'

'It disappoints me, Mr Lomax, that you are willing to give in so easily.'

'I just can't go on taking a client's money when there's no chance of my getting results.'

'Integrity,' she said. 'Such a rare and precious commodity.'

'And it's always given free, never sold.'

'A profound thought. You have a depth, Mr Lomax, which I confess I did not expect.'

'Not depth,' I said bitterly, 'just a

mule-like stubbornness. That's the survival kit for the investigation business.'

'Try not to be cynical. It is a negative response to life which you should strive to eliminate.'

'It's interesting talking to you, Mrs Cassanopolis, but could we move on to discussing just how I can help you?'

'Forgive me,' she said. 'But one so rarely encounters someone with whom one can have an exchange of this kind. And our little talk has been important to me for other reasons. It has enabled me to decide how far I can trust you.'

'Trust me?'

'Yes, Mr Lomax, trust you. You see, our interests could well coincide.'

'I don't follow you.'

'Come now, you must know why Tony Maxwell cultivated his sordid little affair with Miss Morningstar. I must say, you impressed me by getting to her so quickly. Am I correct in assuming, though, that you have not yet found his notebook.'

'I'm looking for a man, Mrs Cassanopolis, not a notebook.'

'Please, no games with me. You are

looking for his notebook or diary because there you hope to find something that will lead you to him. Is that not so?'

'Not entirely. I'm groping for any lead: a letter, a person, a notebook, anything that will help me find him.'

'But you know of his notebook?'

'It would be reasonable to assume anyone collecting information would keep a notebook of some kind.'

She made a tut-tutting noise. 'There is no need for you to be evasive, Mr Lomax. Knowing as you do the kind of venture Tony Maxwell was engaged upon, I am sure you will agree such a book could be important to different people for different reasons.'

'It figures.' I said.

'I want that notebook, Mr Lomax, and I want you to find it for me. There are several men in my employ, but they lack the necessary finesse for a task of this kind.'

'Just handy for the breaking and entry are they, with a bit of the fist and boot business thrown in on the side?'

'I do not understand.'

'My client claims she was visited a couple of nights ago by a bunch of thugs who had her husband with them. She said they beat him up and threatened her.'

'They were searching for the book?'

I just gazed at her and let her question ride.

'I assure you, Mr Lomax, the men who did this thing were not hired by me. But it should convince you of the truth of what I have said: others are seeking the book. Indeed, they may suspect that you or I already have it, and that could place us both in some danger.'

'Who are 'they', and why should 'they' presume that you or I have the book?'

It was her turn to eye me thoughtfully while she decided how much to tell me. Presently she said, 'I have certain business interests in the north. One is always looking for opportunities to expand. Things either grow or die: nothing stays the same. I quickly realised the information Tony Maxwell was gathering could help me further those interests, and I made sure we became acquainted. It will not have passed unnoticed that Maxwell is known to me. If they have not found the book they will assume that I may have it.'

'So that's why Morningstar did the gig at the disco,' I said. 'You wanted Maxwell enticing to your club so you could get acquainted.'

'You're extremely perceptive, Mr Lomax, and quite correct. Miss Morningstar does little favours for me from time-to-time in return for a special service I give her. I do not think she found the task unpleasant; she was foolish enough to become deeply involved with the man.'

'You still haven't told me who 'they' are.'

'Let me just say we are talking about members of a syndicate who have the power to dispense regional franchises in commodities which enjoy considerable demand; men who stand to lose a great deal if the information in Maxwell's notebook is not suppressed.'

'What made you so sure Maxwell would co-operate?'

She gave an amused snort. 'Every man has his price. I paid him in advance for access to any information he might obtain. That notebook is mine, Mr Lomax.'

'This drugs syndicate, where is it based?'

'Who said anything about drugs?'

'Come now, Mrs Cassanopolis. These commodities you talk about can't be anything else.'

'Their organisation works out of Ramford City, but they have interests and outlets in most northern towns,' she said.

I nodded, realising they'd use Ramford's airport to get the stuff in.

'Well,' she said briskly, 'now that we have established a common interest perhaps we can agree terms.'

'I already have a client, Mrs Cassanopolis. What you're suggesting could give rise to a conflict of interest. And anyway, if Maxwell is alive it's certain he still has the book.'

'Nonsense. My interests and those of his wife may not coincide but they certainly do not conflict. She wants a husband: I want his notebook. All I am asking is that if you discover the book during the course of your investigations you turn it over to me after you have made use of it to trace Maxwell. And if he is alive and the book is in his possession I would expect you to reveal his whereabouts to me.'

I eyed her warily.

'I would pay you ten thousand pounds for the notebook, Mr Lomax. Five thousand if you are able to tell me where Tony Maxwell is.'

'I'm sorry, Mrs Cassanopolis. I can't promise anything. Like I said, I already have a client.'

'Integrity is one thing, Mr Lomax crass stupidity quite another. If you are hoping to make me improve my offer you are wasting your time. Ten thousand is all I pay. And I would suggest you reflect on the resources at my disposal before you answer.'

I realised I had to get wise. I couldn't win. I'd get nothing but some more aggravation from her minders if I didn't make the kind of noises she wanted to hear. So I said, 'Okay, Mrs Cassanopolis. The book's no use to my client if she is a widow, and if her husband's still alive I guess you've paid for a peek at it.'

'Ten thousand for the book. Five for Maxwell,' she repeated, then added ominously, 'with or without his notes.'

I rose to my feet.

'Thank you for coming up here to talk with me, Mr Lomax. Let us hope that our arrangement profits us both. I have great confidence in you.'

She unclasped her hands and pressed a button beneath the rim of the table. 'Mr Lomax is coming down now Orville. Would you and Miller escort him to his car.'

I heard a metallic affirmative from a hidden intercom unit.

'How will I contact you?'

'Telephone the club and ask for me,' she said. 'But never leave messages. Any information you have give only to me.'

I nodded. 'I'll keep in touch.'

'Please do, Mr Lomax. I expect to hear from you soon.'

I looked down at her, trying to make something of the lights that glittered in the dark, beady eyes. Small, not quite a dwarf, she had the appearance of a child obscenely aged.

Without another word or gesture, I turned and left her; began my descent from the high tower.

The men called Orville and Miller met me at the bottom door, then led me through the gloom to the sunlight and the car.

'Just watch it, Lomax,' the one with the beard growled. 'We won't be gentle next time.'

They let go of my arms. I shrugged my clothes straight, took the dozen painful steps to the car. I got behind the wheel. The keys were in the ignition. I started the motor and reversed out. Three black Ford Transit vans rounded the final bend in the drive and skidded to a stop on the far side of the car park. The drivers went round the back, opened doors, and about a dozen men tumbled out of each van: tough, weathered looking, the kind you'd expect to find building a motorway.

'Move it Lomax.' The guy with red hair yelled that.

Maybe I was seeing more than I

should. I let out the clutch and headed down the drive. All the way back to Barfield I tried to figure out why a reputable journalist would agree to sell information to some small time crook trying to muscle in on the drugs scene. As the wizened little Greek had said, every man has his price, and perhaps she'd paid him plenty. All the same, my respect for the fourth estate had been badly dented. Another illusion shattered: and I didn't think I had any left.

13

When I got back to the bungalow I made for the sitting room and poured a large Scotch. I swallowed it, began to pour another even before the warm, comforting sensation had started to glow inside me. I let my gaze range over the visible reminders of Orville and Millers' revenge taking: the smashed coffee table, a broken vase, the shattered glass in a photograph frame, up-ended furniture, scattered books and magazines.

I made a half-hearted attempt at tidying the place up, carted the breakages out to the dusbtin; a few things less for me to worry about not dusting and polishing. Possessions aren't something I get uptight about. If I did I wouldn't be in my line of business. It's no game for the acquisitive. At least, not the way I play it. But the broken glass in the frame that held my dead wife's photograph angered me. It somehow made me loathe and despise the thugs who'd violated my home more than the beating up had done.

The phone rang just as the liberal intake of Scotch was beginning to blur the aches and pains. I padded into the hall and lifted the receiver.

'Thank goodness. I've been trying to reach you for hours.' The weak-little-woman voice was Estelle Bergman's.

'You checked out of the motel,' I said accusingly.

'Oh, dear,' she simpered. 'Sorry about that. I know I should have spoken to you about it first, but I got to screaming pitch. I couldn't stand another minute in that drab little room with the inane television programmes and the synthetic food. I had to get out or I'd have gone mad. You're not angry with me, are you?'

'You're free to come and go as you please, Mrs Bergman. I just wanted you there for a while to keep you from harm.'

I began to ask her where she was now, but before I could get the question out she said, 'Have you any news of Carl for me?'

'None,' I said. 'I seem to be getting nowhere fast.'

'But you've had no bad news of him?'

'I've not had any news, Mrs Bergman. In fact I was wondering if you'd care to call the inquiry off. I don't think there are any more leads I can follow. And you'd cut your losses.' I hoped she'd take my last remark as a tactful reminder she'd not had any losses yet; that I was due to some payment.

'Please, please don't say that,' she begged. 'You're my only chance of finding Carl. You must keep on trying for me.'

'There's been some unpleasant developments,' I said. 'I seem to be stirring up a hornet's nest. It could do you and maybe your husband a lot of harm.'

'Surely that only proves there's something to hide. Look, Mr Lomax, I know that wasn't my husband who was buried three days ago. We're so close, so very close. It's not an ordinary marriage. It's something so very special. And because of that I can feel him reaching out to me, telling me he's still alive, crying out for me to find him. You've got to go on helping me.' The telephone somehow distilled all the meaningless inflections from her voice, left only the burning conviction.

'Where are you now?' I asked.

'I phoned a friend . . . Well, more of an acquaintance really, and asked her if I could stay with her for a few days. I told her I was having domestic problems. I don't know why I didn't think of it before. Silly of me. I suppose I was too upset to think.'

'May I ask who this friend is, Mrs Bergman, and where she lives?'

'Oh, yes. Sorry. She's called Cassanopolis. Owns an exclusive country club near Wetherton. I'm staying in her flat in Barfield. Consort Place, opposite Queen's Park.'

I wrestled with the whisky for control of the tiny part of my brain I do my thinking with. 'How do you know this Mrs Cassanopolis?'

'We've had a few drinks parties since we came to Barfield; Carl's friends mostly. She came along to one or two of them.'

'Why her, why not some other guest?'

'Why not? She's a widow. Old and tiny and awfully sweet. She's Greek: I suppose that's what made me remember her.'

'Where are you speaking from?'

'The flat, of course.'

'Are you alone?'

'Yes. The housekeeper's gone. She prepared a meal then left about four. Mrs Cassanopolis said she'd be back from the club around seven.'

I decided to risk talking over the phone. The memory of that wizened, doll-like creature made my voice urgent as I said, 'I can understand you not wanting to be shut up in a motel bedroom, but if you can't stand it I think you should go a long way from here. Pack your bags and clear out.'

'I can't do that.' She sounded bewildered. 'I have to stay in Barfield. Carl might need me. I'd never forgive myself if I wasn't here when he comes back.'

'Mrs Bergman, you may never see your husband again. You must face up to the possibility.' I didn't like giving her that, but I had to try and get her to accept the situation.

'I can't imagine why you had to say such a hurtful thing,' she said coldly. 'My husband's alive, I know he is.'

'Okay, Mrs Bergman, if you say so.' I didn't even try to hide the weariness in my voice. Why should I keep on arguing with the client. It would be her money she was wasting when she got round to paying me.

'Did you ever invite anyone from Ramford City?' I asked.

'Oh dear, the parties seem a long, long time ago. I don't think I remember anyone else. They were all Carl's friends, you see.'

'Try,' I urged. 'An educated professional woman, perhaps.'

'A woman doctor came with her husband to one of the parties. Her husband was a barrister. He was a good deal older than her. But I don't remember their names or where they came from. There were no other women that could be described in that way. In fact, most of the guests were men.'

'Do you recall anything else about her, anything at all?'

I heard her sigh. 'Not really. I think she told me she'd contracted out of the Health Service, practised privately. That's all.'

It wasn't much, just another straw to clutch at. I said, 'I'll keep working at it for another couple of days, Mrs Bergman, if you're sure that's what you want.'

'Oh, I am, Mr Lomax. And I'm so relieved you will.'

'I didn't receive that cheque you promised. I'm clocking up quite a few expenses and a payment on account would be very useful to me at the moment.'

'I really am sorry,' she said. 'There were no cheques left in the book. I'll call at the bank tomorrow.'

I was too weary to press her any more about payment, but I mustered what energy I had left and asked a final question. 'The men who brought your husband back to your home the other night and started beating him up, what were they like?'

'Big. Awfully big.'

'But what did they look like?'

'It was so horrid, my mind's a blank. They were just . . . big.'

I didn't want to put pictures in her head she'd say yes to without thinking, but I had to prompt her or I'd have got nowhere. So I said, 'Bigger than me?'

'Oh, no.' The weak-little-woman voice was back. 'Not as big as you.'

'Was there anything about them you remember? Like scruffy clothes or long hair or moustaches or beards or Ramford accents.'

She gave a fluttery little laugh. 'No, nothing like that. They all wore expensive looking suits. No beards or long hair, but one of them was a coloured man. Why?'

'Just floundering around,' I said.

'Well, I'll say goodbye, Mr Lomax.'

'And you'll not forget the cheque?' I got the words out before I heard the click and the buzzing of the disconnected line, but I don't think she caught the entreaty.

I took the bottle of Scotch into the bathroom and swallowed a few more optic fulls while I tried to soak away the pain Orville and Miller had inflicted. Cassanopolis must have thought it was her birthday when Estelle Bergman rolled up for bed and breakfast, but short of going round to the flat and dragging Mrs Bergman out, there was nothing I could do to make her leave. And I didn't want to scare her out of the place by telling her any more than I had to. Those kind of revelations would have shattered some fond beliefs she held about her blissful union with fornicating Carl, and she wouldn't have thanked me for that. Anyway, I figured it was very much in Mrs Cassanopolis' interests to keep her innocent of the facts and in one piece, at least for the time being. Cassanopolis would maybe regard her as an indemnity she could call on later if I didn't deliver the goods. My initial surprise at Estelle Bergman being acquainted with Cassanopolis had faded. If her husband was doing some kind of deal with the tiny Greek it followed he might invite her to a party they were throwing.

By now, warm bath and whisky were making my pathetic attempts at rational thought a bigger waste of time than usual, so I just abandoned myself to a stupor of total indifference.

14

I visited the reference section of Barfield's Central Library on the way into the office the following morning and looked through the medical directories. It didn't take long to discover that Ramford City boasted only six women doctors, and of that six two were listed as practising in the private sector. A check through the legal directories threw up a barrister called Shardos, the same surname as one of the doctors. I noted down the telephone number and address of her consulting rooms; no private address was given for the woman doctor or her barrister husband.

I got into the office building a few minutes after ten, opened the box behind my slot, and took that morning's pitiful offering with me into Melody's agency. I glanced around her main office. Three girls were pounding the keys but there was no sign of the boss.

I caught the eye of the willowy number with waist length black hair. 'Melody?' I asked.

She nodded towards the back of the room.

I made my way between the desks and machines and went through the open door. Melody stood with her back to me, collating some documents from piles of duplicated sheets laid out on a table.

She turned, startled by the sound of the closing door. 'Thank goodness you've come in.' Relief was audible in her voice.

I let my eyes roam over the white linen suit, the flimsy sandals, the black silk blouse that was cut to keep her temperature down and mine up. I perched on the edge of the desk, trying to work out whether her tan had darkened since yesterday. Against it her eyes flashed like hot sapphires and her hair was pure gold. Somehow I managed to stop myself ogling the combination and said, 'I'm glad somebody's pleased to see me.'

'Somebody,' she snorted. 'Everybody in Barfield wants to see you.'

I braced myself and grinned up at her.

'That smelly debt collector came back yesterday afternoon. He said the garage won't wait any longer; they're starting court proceedings. Your bank manager phoned; he asked me to tell you the question of your car loan and overdraft has been taken out of his hands and the bank would be taking action. And those huge men, the one with the beard and the one with red hair, came looking for you just after you'd gone out. I couldn't make them understand you're hardly ever in and they lounged around the entrance hall until after three.'

I gave her a grateful smile. 'Sorry you're having all this trouble.'

I began to tear open the mail: a final demand, a letter from an industrial client asking me to explain an expenses item on a six-month old account, an office equipment circular and a notice from the bank's solicitors saying they were starting legal proceedings. The bank manager hadn't been bluffing. I reached behind Melody's desk and dropped the lot in the waste paper basket.

'You mustn't do that. Some of them

seemed important,' she said.

I tried hard to look nonchalant. 'I can't do anything about the debts at the moment. Answering letters with more letters is just a waste of time. It's cash they want. I'll clear it all up in a couple of days when the cheques come in.'

Her lips parted. I could see tiny flecks of pink lipstick on her teeth and her eyes were wide and serious as she said, 'You look ill, haggard almost. You'll have to take more care of yourself. Stop leading such a chaotic life.'

She was standing quite close: close enough for me to feel the clean, scented warmth of her body. I grinned down at her. 'I'll try,' I said, 'but I'm not making any promises. Can I use your phone?'

'Sure, help yourself.'

She sighed and turned away, began sorting the papers on the table again.

I checked my notebook, then dialled the Ramford City number listed for Dr Shardos. I listened to the ringing tone, wondering how I could best get my foot in her surgery door, trying to decide whether I should say it was Carl Bergman or his alias, Tony Maxwell, I was seeking.

The line clicked. A refined female voice said, 'Dr Shardos' surgery. Can I help you?'

'I'd like to speak to Dr Shardos,' I said.

'I'm afraid that's not possible. She's with a patient at the moment. If you wish to make an appointment I can arrange it for you.'

'It's a personal matter. An urgent personal matter.'

'May I have your name?' Her voice was cool and wary now.

'Lomax,' I said. 'Paul Lomax. But that won't mean a thing to the Doctor. Tell her . . . tell her it concerns Carl Bergman.'

She asked me to hold the line. It went dead while she talked on another extension. Within seconds she was back saying, 'Dr Shardos has asked me to tell you she cannot be disturbed at the moment, Mr Lomax.'

'But did you mention Carl Bergman?'

'I did. Dr Shardos said she has no recollection of anyone by that name.'

'Can I make an appointment to see her?' I was getting desperate.

'Have we had a letter of referral from your general practitioner, Mr Lomax?' She maintained a deferential tone while she said that, discreetly trying to hide the fact she was being smart.

'It's not a medical matter I want to discuss.'

'Then I suggest you telephone Dr Shardos at her home in about an hour if your business is of a personal nature. Good day, Mr Lomax.' Her calm, firm voice was triumphant.

I pressed the studs in the cradle of the phone and dialled again. Presently a sing-song female voice chirped, 'Directory Enquiries. What town please?'

'Ramford.'

'What name please?'

'Shardos. Dr Shardos. Private number, not her surgery. I don't have the address.'

I listened to the sound of her breathing for a while, then she said, 'I only have one Shardos in the greater Ramford area, but I'm afraid the number is exdirectory.'

'Can you give me the address then?'

'I'm sorry, sir. I can only give information listed in the directory.' The line went dead on me.

I pondered whether to go up to my office or head for the Bergman residence and finish the search I'd started a couple of days earlier. I didn't want to hang around the office any more than I had to: a head on confrontation with debt collectors and sundry creditors was best avoided until I had some cash to make the encounter meaningful. Anyway, Telecom having disconnected the phone, the office was about as much use as a can of castor oil in a dysentery ward. But Melody had been taking a lot of flack on my account. I figured I could hardly walk out and leave it all to her again, so I thanked her for the use of the phone, made some pretence of having to get up there and finish a report, and headed for the stairs.

15

I got behind the desk and slumped down in the swivel chair. Melody was right. I had to get myself organised. Regular meals, eight hours sleep. Who knows, I might even do marquetry, model the Eiffel Tower in matchsticks, embroider a tablecloth; lead a richer, fuller, more cultured life.

The thud of feet on the last flight of stairs and the growl of male voices jerked me out of the reverie. There was no faltering when they reached the landing, they just pushed through the outer office and burst in.

Negro, white man, oriental: a United Nations delegation. I eyed them over the cluttered desk, said nothing.

'Lomax?' The negro asked the question.

I nodded.

Their light-weight suits were hand tailored. The handsome negro was tall, broad shouldered, fastidious; he pulled a blue silk handkerchief from the breast pocket of his blue suit and flicked dust from one of the visitors' chairs. With a grimace of distaste, he lowered himself onto the rexine. The white man was smaller, round faced, chinless, with cold, dead eyes. He flopped down on the other chair without bothering about the dust-off treatment. The oriental leant against the filing cabinet: pale flat face, oiled black hair, massive Sumo wrestler's build. The thin, expensive material of his suit was pulled taut in some places, crumpled in others.

Nobody spoke. They were playing at playing it cool. I looked from one unblinking pair of eyes to the next, then worked my way back again. Their faces were the faces of hard men surviving in a world where the price of survival is a constant readiness to inflict violence and terrible retribution for any slight, real or imagined. A dog-eat-dog world where mercy and honour would be despised aberrations.

I winced inwardly. I was in poor shape after the working over Cassanopolis' heavies had given me the day before. I liked the look of this second batch even less.

'We've heard you're trying to locate a guy called Tony Maxwell,' the white man said presently.

'What if I am?'

'We'll put the questions, Lomax,' the negro's deep voice was cultured.

'You've not found him yet?' the white man asked.

I shook my head. 'I've got nowhere. Nowhere at all.'

'Are you looking for a live man or a dead man?' the negro said enigmatically.

'I have it on good authority he's alive.'

The negro showed me some perfect teeth.

'So you think he's alive but you've not found him yet?' the white man said.

I shook my head some more.

Negro and white man laughed softly. The oriental's face was a mask.

The negro looked disdainfully around the office, contempt showed in the set of his features. 'I'm not surprised you work out of a dump like this. If you're so stupid you can't find Maxwell, business must be bad. I bet you couldn't find a dead skunk in a picnic hamper.'

The white man guffawed at that. The oriental was silent. I wondered if he could understand the language.

With slow, indolent movements, the white man leant forward in his chair, picked up a pile of papers from his side of the desk, made a pretence of flicking through them, then flung them down on the floor. His thin lips were drawn into a sneer and his eyes were challenging me to do something about it.

I stared back. It wasn't easy maintaining a bored-to-death expression in that company.

'We don't like you looking for Maxwell,' the negro said. 'We want you to stop. Now.'

'We?'

'Yes, we. The organisation we represent.'

'Why shouldn't I try and find him?'

'We're not bothered about the finding, just the searching, Lomax. And if you've not found him yet you must be even more stupid than you look.' The white man said that.

'Searching?'

'Searching. You're blundering around, sending out ripples. We don't like that. Our business is very sensitive.' The negro eyed me steadily. He was toying with a heavy gold bracelet. There were plenty of chunky gold rings on his powerful fingers, some with gem stones. The jewellery didn't make him look effeminate.

The white man took out a cigarette lighter, flicked it open and set the jet to give a six-inch flame. He held it beneath the rim of the desk.

'Read any good books lately?' the negro asked.

I raised my eyebrows in a silent question.

'Notebooks, stupid. Like Maxwell's notebook.'

Smoke was rising from the edge of the desk now.

The oriental was enjoying it, getting into the spirit of the thing at last. Slant eyes glittered malevolently and he was showing me his tiny, spaced-out teeth.

'You're a lousy cheap skate, Lomax,' the white man said. 'The desk's only chipboard. Won't even burn; just fizzles and stinks. It's like torching a cat's armpit.

'You have an advantage over me there,' I said.

'Huh?'

'Cat's armpit: I've never torched one.'

He flicked the ligher shut and scowled at me. 'Don't get smart, Lomax. Where's the book?'

'I'm just looking for a guy called Maxwell,' I said. 'I don't know anything about a book.'

'You were looking for Maxwell.' The negro stressed the 'were'.

'Okay,' I said genially. 'I'm not looking for Maxwell. Happy now?'

'The book, Lomax. What about the book?' The negro's voice was soft, menacing.

'You've got it all wrong. I don't know anything about a book.'

'Cassanopolis,' said the white man. 'What do you know about her?'

I shrugged. 'Sounds like a Greek. I

don't know any Greeks.'

'You don't know where Maxwell is, you don't know about his notebook, you don't know who your client's living with. Surely you don't expect us to believe you're as stupid as that, Lomax?' The negro's voice was like the warning growl of an animal.

I linked my hands on the blotter, tried to appear relaxed, all the time searching for some clue to their intentions in the ice fields of cruelty that lay behind the cunning, watchful eyes.

'The notebook: if you have it, or if you know where it is, we want it. It belongs to us,' the white man said.

'I'm not likely to find anything now, am I? Not now that I've stopped looking for Maxwell.'

'Perhaps not,' the negro said. 'But you might just stumble across it. Then again, you may already have it. Or know where it is.'

'I told you,' I snarled, 'I don't know about a notebook. I've just been trying to locate some guy for his ever-loving wife.'

They exchanged sly glances.

The negro said, 'You're so smart,

Lomax, I bet you do brain surgery on the side.'

Even the oriental's face twisted into a faint smile at that; negro and white man laughed out loud.

The negro suddenly stopped laughing. His face hardened. 'If you find the book Lomax, we want to know. Straight away.'

'How can I reach you?'

'We'll contact you.'

'That could be difficult. I'm often out.'

'We'll come looking and we'll find you.' The negro's voice was menacing. 'And forget Maxwell, you're wasting your time.'

'And if I don't?'

The white man leant forward, rested his elbows on his knees. Both hands were wrapped around the cigarette lighter. He pressed the ignite button. Flame spurted, a searing dagger of light. He eyed me through the shimmering heat. 'I won't waste gas on a desk next time, Lomax.'

He killed the flame and slid the lighter into his pocket. As if it was a signal, he and the negro rose to their feet and the oriental pushed himself away from the filing cabinet.

'We'll be in touch,' the negro said.

They strolled arrogantly to the door: expensive suits, hand made shoes, freshly laundered shirts. The oriental was in the rear. As he went through the opening he turned, bared twin rows of tiny, spaced out teeth, then was gone. He'd not uttered a sound. Maybe he was dumb.

I waited until their footsteps were deadened by the carpet on the lower flight of stairs, then went round to the front of the desk, picked up the scattered papers, and dumped them in the waste bin. I got the window open to clear the fumes from the still smouldering desk top, then went across the landing to what the agents laughingly described as 'my own exclusive toilet facilities': a crazed wash-hand basin and a stained pan that some contortionist dwarf of a plumber had managed to squeeze into a cupboard at the top of the stairs. I filled a beaker with water, returned to the office and splashed it onto the smouldering wood.

A small inner voice kept reminding me

Estelle Bergman hadn't paid me a penny yet; that I'd no obligations to honour. I'd already immersed myself up to the nostrils in a drugs racket; one more false move and I'd drown. Rival gangs seemed to be competing for a slice of the action. Cassanopolis heavies were violent in a crude kind of way, but the visiting team were in a different league: I figured they were the guys who'd dropped in on Estelle Bergman the night of the storm. They all wanted her husband's notebook. Maybe Cassanopolis needed it to elbow her way in and the other outfit wanted to use it as a firelighter to make sure things stayed the way they were.

The Bergman business or the creditors? Either way I'd probably get liquidated. The creditors wouldn't make it physically painful: I'd lose the car, the business, maybe even a few personal effects. Then I'd be one more recruit into the growing army of unemployed. If I stayed on the Bergman case I might not get paid and liquidiation, when it came, would be painful and terminal. But it wasn't a certainty. So I decided to ignore the small voice that whispered warnings to me. I pulled the window shut and headed for home where creditors were less likely to call and the phone was still connected.

I guess the blind panic of today always drives away the mindless fear of tomorrow.

16

I parked the Rover on a lay-by near the turn-off into the estate, then walked the remaining two or three hundred yards to the bungalow. I'd seen enough car snatch-back jobs to realise it wasn't wise to take it up to the front door while the bank were suing me for the outstanding loan.

As soon as I got inside the bungalow I blew the dust out of a glass, poured myself the last of the whisky and took it with me to the phone. I checked the Ramford City number, then dialled Dr Shardos' surgery again.

A female voice, younger than the one that had answered that morning, told me I was through to the consulting rooms.

'I'd like to speak to Dr Shardos, please.'

'I'm sorry, she's no longer here. Surgery ends at twelve and then she leaves the premises.'

I injected all the urgency I could into my voice and said, 'I've a very important matter to discuss with her, nothing to do with medicine, could you give me another number I can call her at?'

'I'm sorry, I'm not allowed to do that.'

'Look,' I insisted, 'It's absolutely vital I get some information to her this afternoon. Could you contact her and tell her Tony Maxwell is waiting to talk to her at Barfield six-one-four-five.'

'Well . . . '

I sensed she was going to refuse. 'It's important, Dr Shardos won't be pleased if you don't get the message to her.'

I heard a resigned sigh. 'Very well then. I'll contact her, Mr . . . '

'Maxwell,' I prompted. 'Tony Maxwell.' I gave her the phone number again and the dialling code.

The line went dead. I lowered myself into a chair, stretched out, sipped the whisky.

I didn't have to wait long; less than a finger of Scotch. I grabbed the phone and recited the number.

'Tony. Is that you, Tony?' The woman's

voice was begging me to be Tony.

'Dr Shardos?' I asked.

'Who is this?' she sounded puzzled, angry.

'Lomax,' I said. 'Paul Lomax. I'm a private investigator. I'd like to talk to you about Tony Maxwell if I may, Doctor.'

'Why, you've tricked me,' she gasped. 'How dare you. You told my receptionist you were Tony Maxwell. I don't want to talk to you. I . . . '

I figured she was winding herself up to ring off, so I butted in, 'I've got letters you wrote him, Dr Shardos.'

'Letters . . . you can't have my letters.'

'Intimate letters. The ones you signed Sheba.'

'I . . . I . . . What do you want?'

'Just to talk to you about Tony Maxwell. He's gone missing. I've been hired to find him.'

'I'm sure I can't help you. He's not been in touch with me for weeks. I've no idea where he is.'

'You can never tell, Dr Shardos. Things you may think are completely unimportant could help me locate him.'

I listened to the silence for a while, then said, 'May I come to Ramford and talk with you.' I tried to make my voice gentle and reassuring.

'Oh, I suppose so. If you must. But you'll have to be discreet.'

'I'm in business because I am discreet, Dr Shardos. When can I see you?'

'Tomorrow. Tomorrow afternoon, say about half-past . . . '

'Too late,' I interrupted. 'I need to see you tonight. Tomorrow morning at the latest.'

'Tomorrow morning is out of the question. I hold surgery during the morning. And it's surely too late for you to get to Ramford City today.'

'It's only an hour's drive. I could be there just after six.'

'Oh, very well then.' Irritation was evident in her voice. 'I'll see you at seven this evening. But I can't give you very long. I've another engagement.'

'Shall I come to your home?'

'Certainly not,' she snapped. 'Come to the surgery. I take it you have the address?'

I told her I had and said I'd be there at seven.

I went into the bathroom and washed and shaved away the five-o' clock shadow. I dragged a chair over to the cylinder cupboard, pulled the slender remains of my reserve fund from the back of the cold water storage tank and pocketed the lot.

As I crossed into the bedroom I heard voices, footsteps scraping on the concrete drive, then three long rings on the bell. Slowly and gently, I eased the curtain in the bedroom bay window to one side. Through the narrow gap between cloth and frame I could see two men at the front door. One was a big, shabby looking individual in a crumpled suit; the other smaller, with bristly close cropped hair, a Hitler moustache and eyes bright with zeal. They didn't look the type to be hawking Watch Tower. I guessed it was the debt collector and his apprentice paying me a call.

'He must be out,' the small one said.

'He can't always be out. He's never at his office, never at home. There's no wonder his business is in a mess. If these people got down to some real work instead of swanning around there'd be a lot less bad debt.'

'Let's take a look round the back. We've got to serve the court order today or it'll be out of time.'

Footsteps moved around the side of the house and they began pounding on the back door.

I grabbed the last clean shirt from a hanger, got it on, then used the dressing table mirror while I adjusted my tie.

They were back at the front door now, pounding the plywood and abusing the bell.

I yelled, 'Be right with you,' then dashed to the back door and slipped out. I pulled it shut, locked it, then stepped over the fence into the next garden. I dropped to a crouching position as I passed beneath windows, and went from garden to garden until I was half-way up the cul-de-sac. When I emerged into the street I looked back. They were too busy pumping the bell and calling, 'Are you there, Mr Lomax?' to notice me. I turned and headed for the car.

It was almost seven when I motored into the grimy outer limits of Ramford City. A few minutes later I was cruising slowly along a terrace of elegant Regency houses arranged in a crescent around a fenced park. Mellowed brick, pedimented doors and stone trimmings. The evening sunlight flashed on brass nameplates.

I saw number one-two-six gilded onto a fanlight, slowed to walking pace, then pulled into a gap between a Rolls and a Daimler.

I walked back to the house. There were four nameplates, all listing medical practices. On the top plate Dr Shardos' name had been engraved along with the usual string of qualifications. I tried the door: it was locked. There was a brass bell push set into the fluted pilaster. I pushed the porcelain button long and hard. While I waited I looked through the trees in the small private park to the far sweep of the crescent where shadows were soft in the golden evening light. A quiet place in the heart of the city; a place where you could hear birds sing, smell grass and flowers and trees.

I was reaching out to finger the bell again when a white Jaguar drew up to the kerb. She climbed out almost before the wheels stopped turning. Tall and slender, she was wearing a long sleeved black silk dress. The white lace collar and cuffs would have made it look prim on most women, but not on her. She was filling it to perfection.

She rounded the car and came across the pavement towards me. Thick platinum blonde hair was drawn back from a tanned face. She wore no make-up; she didn't need any. Her cornflower-blue eyes were big, alert and penetrating. Her generous mouth was pressed into a hard line above a firm chin.

'Mr Lomax?'

I nodded, said, 'Good evening, Dr Shardos,' and held out a hand.

She ignored it, brushed past me to the door, slid a key into the latch with long slender fingers. She got the door open and stepped inside. I followed and closed the door. Without a word she walked on down the carpeted hall. Her hair was gathered at the nape of her neck with a bow of black silk.

She led me into a consulting room. Tall windows with blue velvet drapes overlooked a walled garden at the rear of the house. Desk, chairs, table and bookcase were reproduction Chippendale style. The carpet was blue and gold. Only the examination couch struck a jarring note: Chrome and black leather with a neatly folded wool blanket at one end.

She sat, very straight backed, on one of the fragile chairs and inclined her head towards another in a wordless command to sit.

I sat.

'My letters, Mr Lomax, where are my letters?'

I gazed at her. I couldn't fault Carl Bergman's alias Maxwell's taste, it was impeccable. I figured he must have an irresistible appeal to women: the vulnerable coloured kid in the council flat, the extroverted night club singer and now this professional woman, refined, elegant, educated.

'I'd like to talk to you about Tony Maxwell first, if I may, Dr Shardos.'

'There's absolutely nothing I can say that could possibly help you,' she said frostily. The blue eyes raked me up and down. I guessed she was giving me the kind of look she reserved for the lower orders when they were getting out of hand.

'It's often trifling facts or incidents that make the most helpful leads.' I met her shrewd, penetrating stare. She didn't blink or avert her eyes. Presently I said softly, 'Casual remarks have led me to you.'

'You must realise, Mr Lomax, my profession, my marriage, place me in an extremely sensitive position. What guarantee have I got that you'd be discreet and respect my confidences?'

'I'm hired because I'm discreet. If I wasn't I'd not stay in business a week.' I winced inwardly when I said that. All the creditors were closing in for the kill. I probably wouldn't be in business another week.

She crossed her long, black stocking-covered legs, and allowed her back to rest against the fretted back of the chair. Her feet were small, almost out of proportion to the rest of her body. They were tucked into black patent leather shoes with pointed toes. Smooth hands were folded on her lap.

'I don't know you from Adam, Mr Lomax. Your assurances are utterly worthless to me,' she said.

I got my wallet, fished out a card and offered it to her. She made no effort to take it from me, but the slightly raised eyebrows, the disdainful set of the mouth, told me what value she put on my credentials.

'My card, Dr Shardos. I have got proof on me that I am the person named on it.'

She gave an audible sigh, then her slender fingers reached out and plucked the card from mine.

'So you are Paul Lomax and you are a private investigator,' she said irritably. 'That doesn't mean I can trust you. And if I did, which I don't, it doesn't mean I've got to sit here and give you details of my private life.'

'I'm just asking for your help, Dr Shardos,' I kept my voice low and gentle. 'If I don't get it I'll have to quit the case, terminate my inquiries.'

'I really don't think your problems are my concern, Mr Lomax.'

I was getting tired now. Arrogant and unhelpful, she was making me angry. I let it show on my face and in my voice as I said, 'I've incurred a lot of expense, taken a lot of hassle, it's even involved a beating up to get me this far, Dr Shardos. If I don't see the thing through I maybe won't even get paid, and that would open up a whole new vista of problems for me. So don't you think you could help by giving me a little information?'

She sniffed and looked down her nose at me, a smug little smile moving over her lips. 'I'm sorry,' she said, in her cultured voice, 'I'm afraid I can't. And I'd venture to suggest the hassle, as you call it, is an occupational hazard in your grubby business. Your problems are no concern of mine.'

I realised then she wasn't amenable to persuasion. Beauty, education, wealth, privilege; a barely concealed and possibly inbred contempt for the lower social orders, all seemed to make her secure enough to adopt an arrogant, unhelpful attitude. So I ditched the Queensbery rules, decided to play it dirty and said, 'You either talk to me or I have a talk with your husband, Sheba.' I grinned at her.

Her mouth hardened, her eyes became very bright and wary. 'You wouldn't dare.'

'Try me.'

'Your threats are a complete waste of time,' she snapped. 'I've nothing to say to you.'

'Don't give me that, Dr Shardos. You said plenty to Maxwell in those letters. You can't say you know nothing about him after that kind of relationship.'

'How . . . how did you get hold of my letters?'

'You really want to know?'

'Of course,' she snapped.

'From another lady friend of his.'

'Other lady friend . . . he had other women?'

I laughed softly. 'Sure. It's a trail of conquests that's led me to you.'

Her face was ashen now. She was digging her nails into the palm of her hand. 'And he gave my letters to this . . . this woman?'

'He was just careless,' I said. 'She found them in a jacket he left in her wardrobe.'

'You mean he was living with her?'

'On and off.'

'Who is this woman?'

'I said I was discreet, Dr Shardos. I can no more tell you who she is than I could reveal your identity.'

Her shoulders had sagged a little, but her blue eyes, searching and intense, still held mine.

'So how about a little information. I don't want intimate details, just facts that might help me locate him.'

'No.' She almost shouted the word. 'I don't give a damn about your pathetic threats. I'm not discussing any aspect of my private life with you. And if you think going to my husband can help you, you're mistaken. He'd sue you. He wouldn't leave you the lickings of a dog.'

I laughed. 'He'd have to get in the queue.'

She seemed to be recovering fast from the shock of learning she'd only got a part share in Bergman, or Maxwell as she seemed to know him. She threw back her shoulders and said frostily, 'You've not told me why you're trying to trace him.'

'For his wife,' I said. 'She's distracted.'

'Wife? Tony's not married.'

'But surely you knew he was married, Dr Shardos?'

'Of course not,' she snapped. 'And that's not surprising considering all the other things I didn't know about him.'

A discordant note was sounding somewhere. I struggled to drag half-remembered facts through the tangle of worries that cluttered my mind. 'His wife told me you'd been to their home; to a drinks party. You went with your husband. Maybe three or four months ago.'

She sighed. 'My husband and I go to a great many parties, Mr Lomax. Dinner parties, cocktail parties, professional functions. A week later it's all a blur to me. I certainly can't remember parties I went to months ago.'

'But surely you'd remember one in

Barfield,' I said. 'One so far from home.'

'I can't remember a place called Barfield, let alone having been there.'

'As I understand it, you must have met Tony Maxwell at a drinks party in Barfield. I'm surprised you can't remember where and when you first met.'

'Tony Maxwell came to see me here,' she said. 'He told me we'd met before, but I couldn't . . . Look, what is all this,' she snapped, suddenly realising she'd dropped her guard.

'Dr Shardos,' I said gently, 'I don't know what your feelings for Tony Maxwell are or were, but he could be in great danger. He might even be dead. Some small, apparently insignificant thing you might tell me now could save him a lot of pain and trouble.'

'I'm sorry, Mr Lomax,' she said coldly. 'I've told you repeatedly I'm not prepared to discuss the matter with you. The conversation is at an end. Please leave my consulting rooms.'

I glowered at her. She'd completely regained her composure. She was back in the driving seat again. She'd called my bluff about the letters, maybe she didn't even care if her husband knew about the affair. I felt beaten. I was stony broke. I'd driven a hundred miles for a whole load of nothing. A great weariness welled up inside me and spawned an uncontrollable rage. 'You lousy callous bitch,' I snarled. 'You don't care about Maxwell, or his wife, or your husband. All you're bothered about is saving face, making sure your self esteem's not bruised. I'm glad I'm not one of your patients. Judas Priest, I'm glad I'm not your husband. I . . . I'd get you over a chair and beat your backside black and blue.' I paused for breath, glaring hatred and rage at her; a part of my mind had been detached, listening to what I'd been saying like a shocked eaves-dropper.

Her eyes, round with surprise, suddenly softened. For the first time her mouth pulled into a real smile. 'I might not object to that, Mr Lomax.' Her voice was almost a whisper. 'At least you'd be showing you cared. Acting like a man and doing something about it.'

My viciousness hadn't frightened or

angered her. It just seemed to have broken through her arrogant, icy reserve.

'Just because I don't wear my heart on my sleeve doesn't mean I don't have feelings. You probably think a woman in my position has every advantage. But it's not like that at all. You see, only a certain kind of man, and a man from a certain type of background at that, would consider me approachable.' She sighed and looked down at her hands. 'Whether or not I'm naturally drawn to that type of man is another matter. Tony Maxwell wasn't cast in that mould. He was utterly different from any man I'd ever met before. I was just a woman to him, not some repressed workaholic doctor, a make-you-well machine. When he looked at me all he ever saw was a woman.'

She raised her eyes to mine again. She didn't have to remind me she was a woman. The way she wore her hair, the absence of make-up, the severe black dress and shoes and stockings: all the tricks she played to hide her sex and convey a detached professional image, weren't working.

'Have you any idea where he might be?'
I asked.

She shook her head. 'I'm afraid not.'

'He could be in a lot of trouble, Dr Shardos.'

She sighed and said, 'I'm sure you're right. I knew there was something wrong the last time I saw him.'

'When was that?'

'Eight days ago. He called to see me here.'

'You're certain it was eight days ago?'

'Completely. I'll never forget it. He interrupted my surgery. It was more than a little embarrassing. I asked him never to do that.'

'Did you know he was gathering information on the drugs scene?'

'He was what?'

'Researching. For a series of articles on drug abuse. You knew he was a journalist, a writer?'

She laughed. 'He was full of surprises, Mr Lomax, but I would never have thought he was a writer, not in a million years.'

I shrugged. 'His wife told me one of the

Sunday papers had made him an advance on the series.'

'Sunday paper ... advance?' She looked puzzled. 'Are you sure we're both talking about the same man?'

I took out the photograph Estelle Bergman had given me and handed it to her.

She glanced down at it, then passed it back. 'That's Tony all right. But I'd never have guessed he was a writer. He didn't seem to be the intellectual type. He was such a sensual man.'

'How did you think he earned his living?'

'He told me he was a rep for a drugs company. I presumed that's why he called at the surgery in the first place.'

'Do you specialise?'

She was looking at me blankly, chewing her lip. Her teeth were large and very white. She seemed lost in thought.

'Specialise, Dr Shardos?' I prompted.

She gave me her attention again. 'Sorry, Mr Lomax. Yes, I specialise in drug abuse. I've done a considerable amount of research into its long term physiological effects. That was before I contracted out of the Health Service, of course.'

'Presumably you're regarded as an expert in the field?'

'I wouldn't know about that. I've written articles for the journals and a lot of cases are referred to me.'

'But anyone involved professionally with drug abuse would know about you?'

'You could say that.'

'Did Tony Maxwell ever discuss the drugs business with you?'

She thought about that one for a while before she said, 'Not really,' then she frowned and seemed uneasy as she went on, 'the only thing he ever asked me to do was to write him prescriptions for his own company's products. He said it helped him with his monthly sales quotas.'

I looked at her steadily. My eyebrows hadn't lifted more than a millimetre. All the education, poise and assurance hadn't stopped her being suckered by a top class con-artist.

'What company did he represent?'

'Synarcot. They synthesise the opiate

drugs and manufacture the usual range of amphetamines. They're very good.'

We eyed one another for a few moments in the silence of that elegant room while thick carpet, velvet drapes and polished wood soaked up the last of the golden light. Her resigned sigh seemed loud in the silence. I guess the pennies were dropping.

'He's upset some ruthless people, Dr Shardos. I suspect he's found out too much about the way a big distribution syndicate operates.'

Two lines creased her high forehead. 'It seems a little far fetched. Are you sure about all this?' she said.

'They know I'm looking for him. I've had some heavy threats from the big operator and a proposition from a smaller outfit that wants to carve itself a slice of the action.'

'But why threaten you?'

'Tony Maxwell kept some kind of notebook. That's what's causing the excitement. The people controlling things probably want to burn it; the other outfit see it as a key that can unlock the door for them.'

Alarm showed in her eyes. 'Could you have been followed here?'

'No, Dr Shardos,' I said gently. 'I'm pretty sure no one followed me. But if I can trace you they can too. Maybe more easily; their resources are greater than mine. And, like I said, they're ruthless, utterly ruthless.'

The alarm became fear. 'Do you think I could become involved in all this?'

'It's possible.'

She looked at me, wide eyed, her body tense. 'I wasn't trying to deceive you when I said the letters don't bother me. My husband's a very civilised, understanding kind of man and I could have handled that situation. But I don't feel the same about being involved with these . . . these racketeers. Something like that could finish me professionally and socially. And there's my husband: how would a barrister cope with a wife embroiled in trouble of that kind?'

'They only want one thing, Dr Shardos: the notebook. If it exists at all. Do you have it, or do you know where it is?'

'I don't know whether I have it or not,' she said. 'When Tony last came to see me he was very nervous. I'd never seen him that way before. He was always so relaxed and easy going. He gave me two large envelopes and asked me if I'd take care of them for him, just for a while.'

'Do you know what was in these envelopes?'

'I've no idea. Papers I presume. They were very bulky. Tony made it clear the contents were extremely valuable to him.'

'Do you have them here?'

She shook her head. 'No. I kept them here a couple of days then took them to the bank and had them stored in a safe deposit box. I became uneasy about having them in the surgery.'

'The syndicate employs some nasty little sadists, Dr Shardos. An acid job's the favourite frightener for a woman.'

Fear was tightening the muscles of her face. 'Do you think I should hand the parcels over to the police?'

'I think you should get rid of them fast, but giving them to the police could cause you problems.'

'I . . . I don't understand.'

'Maybe there's something in there that could link you with Tony Maxwell. Something embarrassing, illegal maybe. You just don't know.'

I looked at her without speaking for a while, then said gently, 'Why not hand them over to me, Dr Shardos. The contents might help me locate him for his wife. And if anyone comes to you I wouldn't care if you let them know I had the envelopes. They know I'm looking for him, and that way you'd be in the clear, out of it all.'

'How could I trust you? You've already threatened me with the letters. How do I know you won't do the same with whatever is inside the packets?'

'No problem. You get the envelopes from the bank, bring them back here and take out whatever you want. All I ask is that you let me look over anything that might help me find Tony Maxwell.'

'And what about the letters you already have?'

I looked her straight in the eye. 'I don't have any of your letters, Dr Shardos. I've never even seen one. I was told about them by the woman who found one in Tony Maxwell's jacket. She said she'd destroyed it. I really searched her place but I couldn't find it. I think she was telling the truth.'

'You're very resourceful, Mr Lomax. There was no address, no name,' she blushed faintly, 'or at least, not my real name.'

'It was something the woman who found the letter said. And his wife remembered a woman doctor with a barrister husband at one of their drinks parties. It wasn't difficult to narrow down the field.'

She gave a brisk little sigh that indicated she'd reached a decision. 'Very well, Mr Lomax, I'll go along with your suggestion. On condition you come with me to the bank. Some of the things you've said . . . the acid . . . I don't want to be alone when I have the envelopes.'

'Sure,' I said. I let my gaze wander from the drawn back platinum-blonde hair to the small black shoes. 'It'll be my pleasure, Dr Shardos.'

'Can I offer you a drink before you go?'

'I'd appreciate it.'

'Sherry, Scotch, brandy?'

'A Scotch would be fine.'

She rose, went over to the bookcase, and brought out a decanter and a couple of glasses. She poured a couple of generous shots, carried one over to me, then leant against the desk. The cut of the dress somehow emphasised her beautiful legs and imparted an elegant slenderness to the whole of her body. I'd got round to thinking she could run her stethoscope over me any time when she said, 'What are they like?'

'They?'

'His wife and this . . . this other woman.'

I shrugged, turned the corners of my mouth down in a non-committal gesture.

'Are they attractive?'

'You could say that.'

'Are they . . . beautiful?'

'They're both very beautiful, Dr Shardos.'

She raised her glass to her lips; lips that had parted in a replete, mysterious smile. 'Here's hoping Tony shows up soon,' she said.

17

I didn't leave Ramford City that night. I figured it was pointless returning to Barfield just for a few hours. For one thing I couldn't afford fuel for the two hundred mile round trip. For another, with all the creditors closing in for the kill I figured I was best out of the way. Instead I had a beer, ate a plastic tray full of something indescribable from a Chinese take-away, then bunked down in the car which I'd left in a multi-storey park.

Dawn had me wishing I'd cossetted myself a little more. Limbs stiff and aching, stomach dyspeptic, I looked and felt like a corpse after a cut-price embalming job. I bought a bar of soap and some disposable razors at a news-agents, then made my way to the railway station. I got a platform ticket, found the toilets and washed and shaved. The mirror was fly blown, the basin cracked and stained, the water tepid. I went into the buffet, sampled a couple of bacon rolls and killed time drinking coffee and reading newspapers.

★ ★ ★

It was cool inside the massive city bank. Built in the classical style, with a ceiling just below cloud level, they must have worked out a couple of marble quarries putting the place together. An armoured glass and aluminium security barrier had been fixed along the top of the old walnut counter. It didn't look any more out of place than a handlebar moustache would have done on the manager's wife. Cashiers were dealing unhurriedly with the opening crush of customers. It was the kind of place where you were made to feel they were doing you a favour allowing you to make a deposit there.

I positioned myself behind a rack of pamphlets where I could view the entrance door and the full length of the counter. I flicked through a leaflet, began reading how much they wanted to help me with my unexpected bills. When I looked up again she was joining one of the shorter queues. She wore a sleeveless yellow cotton dress gathered at the waist by a thin gold belt that matched her sandals. Her hair wasn't drawn back now. It was falling around her bare, brown shoulders in silver-gold waves. She carried a shopping bag as I'd suggested. Her eyes were hidden behind dark glasses.

I glanced around the banking hall. Everything and everyone seemed normal. She was edging her way towards the cashier. I left the rack of pamphlets and strode towards her. She turned the dark glasses on me and her mouth pulled into a nervous little smile, then she looked back towards the counter. I stopped by a marble column and watched her. She leant towards the grille, spoke a few words, then the man behind the counter left his pitch and wandered across the business area of the bank.

Dr Shardos had to wait about five minutes before he returned. I saw her pull some bulky envelopes from her end of the security chute, drop them in the bag and drag the zip over.

She walked towards me. The black, professional-woman uniform she'd worn the previous day hadn't managed to keep many secrets, but she was as eye catching as a fire in a dynamite factory in that skimpy yellow dress. Before she reached me I moved to the entrance door, slipped through and held it open. She joined me in the lobby and we stepped out onto the hot pavement.

'My car's parked round the side of the bank,' she said, in a tight nervous voice.

We turned into a side street and headed down a line of parked cars. Sun glared back from windscreens and brightwork; the road and pavement shimmered in the heat.

'Would you carry the bag, Mr Lomax? I'd rather you took charge of it.'

'Sure,' I said, and as I reached out for it all four doors of the Mercedes we were passing crashed open and trouble spilled out.

She gave a little squeal, dropped the bag and ran.

I kicked it hard down the street then hurled my body against the front door of the car and trapped the head of the guy who was climbing out. He started screaming. The sound must have distracted the man who'd emerged from the rear door because he never even saw the punch I slammed into his throat.

I dashed for the bag, got it under my arm and kept on running. I could hear the two other men following. I made a right and turned down the rear of the bank. I sensed one of them was gaining on me; his pounding feet and hoarse, laboured breathing were loud behind me. I saw a narrow opening up ahead. I half jumped, half slid, across the bonnet of a car and spurted down it. The sudden manoeuvre confused the opposition long enough for me to gain a ten pace lead, then I heard his footsteps echoing in the passage, closing on me again. I burst out into sunlight and shoppers. On the far side of the crowded street a bus ground to a stop. I weaved through three lanes of traffic and moved round the bus. I heard the hiss that signals hydraulic doors closing and forced the bag between rubber gummed jaws. Sensors sprung the doors open again. I clambered aboard as the bus lurched off.

I could see my gasping, red-faced pursuer standing by the far kerb. His companion emerged from the passage and joined him. Sweat had formed dark patches under the arms of their expensive, light-weight suits. They watched the bus pull away; fists clenched, eyes hot and angry.

A couple of stops later I got off the bus, flagged down a taxi and dashed to the multi-storey car park as fast as the driver would take me. I figured they might know I'd left my transport there, and I had to get away from the place before they organised themselves and drove over.

I rode the battered lift up to the level above the one where I'd parked the car, then crept back down the stairs. I peered through a round window in the fire door that sealed off the landing. Apart from fifty or sixty cars the place looked deserted. I moved out over the oil stained concrete to the Rover, the door thumping backwards and forwards on its spring behind me. I climbed inside the car, threw the bag on the floor, and headed back to Barfield.

I kept to the secondary roads just in case they were having the motorway watched. Ten miles out of Ramford City I pulled onto the forecourt of a village pub and slit the envelopes open. They were packed with used twenties, about six thousand pounds in all. In one of the envelopes, a cheap notebook had been sandwiched between the bundles of paper money. Dog-eared and used looking, it was half-full of crabbed handwriting. Names of people and places, delivery times and amounts: a detailed picture of a nationwide drugs network and its links with Europe and the East. Carl Bergman, or Tony Maxwell as his conquests knew him, had been painstaking and thorough. Leafing through it all, I could understand the syndicate being desperate to get their hands on it. What surprised me was they'd not tried harder to beat me to the book. Or maybe they'd just followed me all the way, used me to do the leg-work for them. I crammed the cash back in the envelopes, locked them in the glove compartment, then lifted the carpet on my side of the car and hid the notebook under it.

The journey back to Barfield took a couple of hours along the minor roads that meandered through villages and small townships. All the time I was trying to figure out where to go when I got back to town. The syndicate could find me at the office or the bungalow; They'd probably got them under surveillance by now. I needed a place and some time to think. I'd still not had any bright ideas when I closed on Barfield, so I decided to head for the Bergman residence on Mount St Joseph and stay there, at least until nightfall.

I parked the car down the side of the house where it was well hidden beneath the sweeping fronds of a willow tree. I rang the bell and waited, just to be sure Estelle Bergman hadn't returned home. No one answered, so I fished out the bunch of fire-scarred keys and let myself in.

The place was cool and still and seemed to be just as I'd left it when I broke off my search a couple of days earlier. I scooped up newspapers and letters, dumped them on a hall table, then walked through to the sitting room. A brass carriage clock on the mantelpiece showed one-thirty. I poured myself a generous measure of whisky, swallowed it, then treated myself to another. I took it with me to the phone and dialled Melody's number. One of her girls answered; said she'd fetch her.

I heard the phone scrape along the desk, then an angry voice said, 'Where on earth have you been, Paul?'

'How are things at the front?'

'Front,' she exploded, 'we're right in the middle of a battlefield here, and it's your war. The bailiffs have been. They've taken the table and chairs out of your waiting room and the filing cabinets out of the office. They left your desk and chair, said they were unsaleable. I can't tell you how embarrassed I was.'

'And?' I sighed.

'A sauve black man and a white man

with lecherous eyes came asking for you.'

'Lecherous eyes,' I said. 'Do they go with wandering hands?'

'Don't, Paul. I'm not in the mood for funny remarks after the trouble I've had this morning.'

'Anything else?'

'Someone called you about an hour ago. He said you had to phone Barfield four-nine-three-seven before two. He said if you didn't phone before two you and the Bergman woman would be very sorry.'

I didn't answer her. I was letting that one sink in, trying to work out what it might mean.

'Paul . . . Paul, are you alright?'

'Sure. I'm fine, Melody. Absolutely fine.'

'You're in trouble, aren't you?' Concern was diluting the anger and reproach in her voice now.

'Nothing I can't handle,' I said nonchalantly, but deep down I was scared I might be too shattered, too stupid, too senile to handle this situation.

I thanked her and signed off, then

pressed the studs in the cradle and dialled the number.

After a couple of rings, a man's voice snapped, 'Lomax?'

'That's me.'

'The book. We know you've found it. We want it.'

'So what?' I put a sneer in my voice.

'So if you don't deliver it fast, your client gets hurt. We've got her here, Lomax, and she's going to be very upset if you don't get that book to us.'

'How do I know you've got her there?'

'Easy,' the voice said, 'I'll put her on.'

'Mr Lomax, Mr Lomax, is that you?' The weak-little-woman voice, whimpering with terror, was unmistakable.

'I'm here, Mrs Bergman.'

'Come and get me,' she whimpered. 'Come quickly.'

'Are you okay?' I asked.

'They've pushed me around and brought me to this dreadful house that's full of . . . '

'Satisfied, Lomax?' The man was back on the line.

'Okay, so you've got Mrs Bergman, but

I can't give you the book because I don't have it.'

'Orchard Street, Lomax. You know where that is?'

'Sure, it's some way behind the railway yards.'

'Number thirty-eight; fifteen minutes. Be there, Lomax.'

18

Orchard Street was, and still is, the heart of Barfield's red-light district. Asians, blacks, impoverished whites, the town's ladies of joy, all make their homes in the derelict terrace houses. I parked the Rover some distance away. Six thousand pounds was still locked in the glove compartment, the book was under the rug; there hadn't been time to find a safer hiding place.

I took a short cut through some railway arches and across a demolition site where pink willow herb grew between mounds of rubble and the tall grass was scorched and brown. Rainfall hit an all-time low that summer, and that afternoon was no different from a couple-of-dozen others that had gone before: white hot sun blazing out of a sky that was as clear and bright as a nun's eyes. The shirt I'd slept in was soaked with sweat, my suit crumpled, shoes down-at-heel and scuffed. Gritty-eyed and dog-tired, I felt as alert and resourceful as a meths drinker in a terminal coma.

Frizzly hair, black faces; turbans, brown faces; I met them all on the way to Orchard Street. Number thirty-eight wasn't going to make the house-beautiful magazines. A rotting mattress and the charred remains of some discarded furniture lay in a small front garden that was choked with weeds. Weathered and peeling, the place hadn't seen a lick of paint since Queen Victoria's diamond jubilee. Cheap nylon curtains obscured the windows, and the only new-looking thing was a large, illuminated bell push: I guess that needed replacing once, maybe twice a week. I tramped up worn steps and rang the bell.

The curtain in the side window of a bay twitched to one side. A couple of seconds later the door opened. The oriental, one of the gang who'd paid me a call at the office, was standing in the dingy hall. Eyes glittering behind puffy slits in sallow flesh, he beckoned me on with a movement of his head. I stepped inside. He shut the door, bolted it, then led me into a back room.

The coloured guy and the white man, the other members of the team, were lounging in old armchairs. The remains of a meal were strewn over a kitchen table. Cigar smoke, garlic, grease and male sweat gave the room a fragrance Yardley wouldn't want to bottle. Dusty curtains were shutting out the sun and a naked bulb was struggling to relieve the gloom.

'You've been busy, Lomax,' the negro said in his deep, cultivated voice.

I just stared at him, said nothing. He'd spread a clean sheet over the greasy armchair before he'd lowered his elegant, fastidious frame into it. His gold rings and bracelet gleamed softly in the dim light, a light that somehow heightened the contrast between his white teeth and black skin.

'We lost you once or twice,' he went on, 'but we know you went with some woman to a Ramford City bank and got Maxwell's book. We want that book, Lomax. Now.'

'Where's Mrs Bergman?' I grated.

'She's here. She's okay.' The white man said that.

'Let me see her. When I know she's okay I'll talk about books.'

'You're in no position to bargain, Lomax.' The negro said. 'We're going to get the book, no matter what we have to do to you or the woman.'

'It's not too much to ask. Just let me see my client. Then we'll talk.'

White man looked at black man, caught some wordless assent, then glanced at the oriental and jerked his head towards the door.

The oriental padded out. A minute later I heard shoes clattering down stairs, the door swung open and Estelle Bergman was pushed through.

'Thank God you've come,' she whimpered. Tears were overflowing from the huge green eyes, red hair was in disarray, lipstick smeared, dress crumpled. She crossed over, rocking unsteadily on high heels, and snuggled into my chest. I wrapped an arm around her.

'You okay?' I asked.

'They've not hurt me, but they've been

unspeakably coarse. I . . . I want to go now.'

Black man and white man guffawed.

'She wants to go now,' mimicked the white man in a shrill falsetto. 'Listen, stupid, you'll go when Lomax hands over the book. And if we don't get it you'll stay for keeps, join our little fun palace.'

'Where is it, Lomax?' the black man growled.

'Like I said, I don't have it. This afternoon I posted it to myself. Second class. It won't arrive at the office until Monday.'

The black man rose from the chair. Shoulders hunched and menacing, features distorted with anger, he pushed his face close to mine. 'You did what, Lomax?' Garlic stained his breath.

'Posted it,' I said. 'To myself.'

He smashed the back of his hand into my face. We glared at one another across a gap narrow enough for me to smell some aromatic deodorant that had been soured by his sweat. I could hear Estelle Bergman sobbing, feel her clutching frantically at my arm.

The black man grabbed me by the lapels. 'You're lying, Lomax.'

I shook my head. 'I can't give you what I don't have. You can collect it Monday.'

'You're a dirty liar,' he snarled. 'Sid can torch the truth out of you.' He dragged Estelle Bergman off my arm and shoved me back into a chair.

The white man's eyes glittered. He took his cigarette lighter, made a long knife like flame, then said, 'Get your shoes off, Lomax.'

I heard a phone shrilling.

'Off, Lomax.'

He crouched down, grabbed my foot. I drew my leg back. He stumbled forward and my foot pressed into his chest. I rammed my leg straight. He skittered across the room and crashed into the table. Crockery fragmented into white shards on the linoleum.

The door swung open as the negro closed in on me. I heard a hoarse voice yelling, 'They're coming. Four van loads. Black Ford Transits. They've just driven down Ellison Street.'

'Get these two upstairs,' the negro

snapped. 'Sid, get the shooters.'

The message bearer grabbed Estelle Bergman and pulled her through the door. The oriental lifted me effortlessly out of the chair and shoved me after her. They bundled us up two flights of stairs, then pushed us into an attic room at the back of the house. The ill-fitting door shuddered as they dragged it into the frame, then I heard bolts thudding home. I guess it wasn't the first time they'd incarcerated problems in there.

The sun burned through a rectangle of dirty glass let into the slope of the roof, turning the confined space into a furnace. I glanced around. An old iron bed with a stained mattress, a wicker linen basket and a heap of filthy rags were the only contents.

I looked at Estelle Bergman. Her whole body was trembling, her eyes were glazed with fear and shock. I got my arm around her, led her to the bed, and we sat down.

'What ... what's happening,' she faltered.

'Some other gang making trouble,' I said. 'They may even have come over to grab us. Could be Mrs Cassanopolis' boys. I saw black Ford Transits when I went to the club.'

She covered her face with her hands and began to sob. 'Oh God,' she whimpered, 'I wish I'd never let Tony get me involved in all this. They'll kill us. I know they'll kill us.'

I struggled to organise scattered thoughts, get my brains out of neutral. The mob were busy with other things now. I'd never have a chance like this again.

'Stand up a moment,' I said, and helped her to her feet.

I half lifted, half dragged the bed across dirty boards and wedged it against the door, then crossed over to the wall between that house and the next, crouched down beneath the lowest part of the sloping roof and began to pound the ceiling with my fist. Old plaster showered down exposing the laths beneath. I smashed away the thin strips of wood, then got to work on the slates. Fragile with decay, they needed no coaxing; I heard them slither down the roof. Sunlight was pouring in now, and with it the echoing sounds of shouting men, revving engines, slamming doors. I scrabbled feverishly with my hands, enlarging the opening. Then I stood up, put my shoulder against the battens that had supported the slates and heaved. Dry, rotten wood cracked apart and my head and chest were above the roof.

I reached over, cleared a patch of slates on the far side of the party wall, then climbed out. It seemed a rocket ride above the tiny back yard. I stamped on exposed laths and plaster, smashed a way through, then dropped down into the next house. I looked around. Three single beds had been crammed into the tiny attic room. A brass statue of Shiva was resplendent on a gaudily decorated tin trunk. I put the six-armed man on one of the beds and dragged the trunk beneath the hole. I stood on it, got most of my body above the line of the roof, then called Estelle Bergman over. I heard a shuffling sound, then her pale face was looking up at me. She remained in a crouching position, too scared to put her head out of the opening.

'I . . . I thought you'd left me,' she said tearfully.

I ignored the insult and said, 'Stand up so I can lift you out and over here.'

'I can't,' she gasped. 'I just can't. I'm too scared of heights and . . . ' Her voice was rising in pitch. She seemed to be going hysterical on me.

'Come on,' I urged, 'I'll hold you. I won't let you fall.'

'It's no use. I'm petrified. I won't do it, I . . . '

I heard a pounding on the door I'd wedged shut with the bed. Someone was yelling obscenities.

It was as if the room had caught fire. She rose out of the roof like a beautiful jack-in-the-box, reaching towards me. I got my hands under her arms and lifted her out, clasped her against me, then drew her down into the adjoining house.

I took her hand. We dashed out of the room and down the stairs to the first landing where a couple of Sikhs were moving towards us.

I pointed to Mrs Bergman, 'Sister,' I said. 'Men took her, kept her prisoner in room next door.'

Dark eyes flashed, moustaches and beards bristled. 'Very bad men in that house,' said one severely.

'Many bad women, too,' said the other, his voice betraying a certain longing.

I got my wallet, found three tenners and held them out. 'Some damage to roof,' I said. 'Pay for repairs.'

A brown hand darted, cobra like: the notes vanished.

They looked at one another, spoke fast, making sounds like a gorilla drowning in a swamp. Then the taller of the two looked at me and said, 'Guptil take you down, show you back door. I go up, stop bad men.'

We followed the swarthy, turbanned figure. Big-eyed kids and sari-clad women, old and young, stared as we passed through. The Sikh led us out of the back door, across the concrete yard, through a gate into a high-walled alleyway. He pointed, spoke words I couldn't under-stand, then left us.

We ran. I heard a hoarse voice yell my name. I looked back. The white man was standing through the hole in the roof, sighting a rifle on us. I pushed Estelle Bergman against the wall and leaped after her. The gun started to bark, bullets whined as they ricochetted off the crumbing brickwork. We raced on, shielded by the wall, then dived to the right at a crossing in the alleyway. I glanced back; the man had left the roof. Fifty yards more and we burst out into another mean street. I grabbed her arm, we ran over the road and into an alleyway on the far side. We crossed four streets of shabby houses in that way until, beyond a ramshackle clutter of allotment gardens, I could see the railway arches. We followed the line of a fence made from old doors, corrugated iron, rail track sleepers, then plunged into tall grass and weeds on the demolition site.

'Stop. You've got to stop,' she gasped. 'I can't run anymore.'

I let her sink down into the grass and flopped down beside her. We lay there, fighting for breath. I saw she'd lost her shoes; her feet were cut and bleeding. I could hear the distant sounds of shouting and what I took to be gunfire. Then, closer at hand, fast cars approaching. I got on my knees and looked over the vegetation. Police cars and vans were heading along the road that bordered the waste land, then turning up towards the houses.

'We'd better go,' I said. 'Before they start crawling all over the place.'

'I can't. My feet . . . ' she whimpered.

'The car's parked just through those arches. I'll help you.'

'It's no use. I can't go another step.'

I reached down and lifted her to her feet. She made little squeals and moans of protest. I put her over my shoulder, fireman's lift style, and ran until we were hidden beneath a vault of slime-covered brick. I lowered her onto her feet. She ran her arms round my neck and hung on to me, almost a dead weight. I looked back across the sunlit wasteland towards the allotments and the road, but saw no one.

Thoughts were scurrying down the corridors of my mind, taking on shape and form: the tiny Greek and her fat manager, the visit to Morningstar, things

Dr Shardos and Estelle Bergman had said, my half-finished search of the house, the secret laughter of the mob when they paid me a call. Like the tumblers of a well oiled lock, it all dropped into place and I was pushing open the door.

I wrapped my arm around Estelle Bergman, eased the weight off her feet, and we limped on.

'Where are you taking me?' she said, when we were sitting in the car.

'Back to Mount St Joseph. You'll be safe there now the police have started to get in amongst it all.'

'My husband, have you any news of my husband?' Her tired voice was without hope.

'I think so.'

Her body stiffened. She turned wide eyes on me. 'You . . . you know where he is?'

'I'm almost certain.'

'Then take me to him. For Heaven's sake take me.'

'I'll take you to him, Mrs Bergman,' I said grimly. 'But first we'll go to your place and talk.'

19

Beautifully bedraggled, make-up smudged by tears and exertion, red hair in disarray, she curled up in the corner of the huge leather chesterfield. Her green eyes were big and bright, her generous mouth trembling with shock, or maybe apprehension at what was to come. I was struggling to organise my thoughts, trying to decide how best to handle Estelle Bergman and the whole lousy situation. I badly needed a drink, and I knew I had to make her have one too.

'Let me get you a whisky,' I said.

'I don't want a drink. Why are you torturing me like this. Why can't you just take me to my husband?'

'I'm sorry, Mrs Bergman, but we've got to talk first.'

'Oh, very well then,' she said tearfully. 'Get me a whisky and get it over with.'

I poured a couple of extra large ones, handed her a glass, then wedged myself in the opposite corner of the chesterfield. I gazed at her, groping for the right words, words that would steal up on her and take her unawares. But weariness defeated me, so I gave up trying to be smart and said, 'The man you hired me to find wasn't your husband, was he, Mrs Bergman?'

'I . . . I don't know what you mean,' she faltered. It was her weak-little-woman voice. She was staring at me like a frightened child stares at an angry father.

'You conned me, Mrs Bergman. I guess you had to. If you'd told me the truth I'd never have taken the case and you knew that, didn't you?'

I waited for some response, but she just stared at me; lips trembling, eyes wide and scared.

'That's why you had to fabricate the clever little tale about your husband being a writer. A guy researching the drugs scene, someone using a false name and unorthodox methods the police would frown on. You couldn't have reported Maxwell missing to the police, not in a million years. If they'd ever found him they wouldn't have handed him back until you were both too old to care.'

'Why are you being so beastly to me?' she whimpered. 'Why can't you just take me to him?' Her chin trembled. Tiny fingers with vermilion nails brushed away the tears.

'Because I want to get at the truth,' I said. 'After conning me into looking for some small-time crook who was trying to muscle in on the drugs racket, I think you owe me that much, Mrs Bergman.'

'You seem so big and clever and smart I'm surprised you need to ask me anything,' she said.

'Don't you think it's about time you skipped the weak-little-woman act, Mrs Bergman?'

Wide-eyed, she covered her open mouth with her fist, as if stifling a scream, then drew her legs even more tightly under her body. It was Little Red Riding Hood telling Big Bad Wolf how scared she was.

'Please, Mr Lomax, please don't be beastly to me. It was dreadful of me to play tricks on you like that, but I love him so much, I had to find him.'

'And how did you meet Maxwell, this guy you love so much?'

'At a business dinner here. My husband invited him. He used to invite all the guests.'

'Let me guess,' I tried to keep the bitterness out of my voice, 'your husband worked for an outfit called Synarcot?'

She nodded. 'He was the managing director of their U.K. subsidiary.'

'Surely you realised what Maxwell was doing?'

'I'm not very clever, Mr Lomax. I don't understand business. I just . . . just loved him. I know it was wrong, but I couldn't help it. He was so attentive and tender and passionate. It was a . . . a wonderful ecstacy just being near him.'

'So ecstatic you had your husband roasted alive, maybe?'

'No, no, no!' The words exploded in three, breathless little screams. 'How could you say that. I know I'm bad, very bad, but I'd never . . . ' Her face crumpled. The renewed flood of tears carried more mascara down her cheeks.

'But Maxwell was living here with you,

wasn't he, Mrs Bergman? Your husband had cleared out. And that newspaper and other junk you mixed with the things in your husband's brief case, you must have got that from Maxwell's pockets, not your husband's. It was Maxwell who stood beneath the trees and stared up at the house; Maxwell who was brought back here by the gang the night of the storm.'

She didn't deny anything, just buried her face in her hands, huddled into the corner of the chesterfield. Then words began to tumble out between sobs, and she said: 'All that linked me with Carl Bergman was a marriage licence, a silly piece of paper. He was only interested in his work and I was no more to him than a hostess for his boring business dinners. Tony was the friend and lover and husband that Carl never was. So I only told you a teeny-weeny little lie, Mr Lomax. In fact, what with Carl's death and Tony disappearing when I needed him most, I was so confused I just told you what I felt. I didn't even think it was a lie.' She looked up, green eyes huge under long dark lashes. 'Anyway, how did you find out about Tony and me?' she sobbed.

I eyed her steadily. Maybe she'd never really grown up inside; maybe she was still just a kid crying to avoid punishment or to get what she wanted. I decided there was no point distressing her by revealing more than I had to, so I just said, 'Like always it was the small things: the way the keys you gave me didn't open doors they should have opened, the unguarded remarks the people who knew him made. And that includes you, Mrs Bergman, you called him Tony when we were locked in the bedroom, although it didn't register at the time. Your fictitious journalist husband selling himself out to Mrs Cassanopolis didn't ring true either. I don't imagine any self-respecting journalist would sell information that way. And what about Cassanopolis? I bet you knew her through your lover, Maxwell. I bet she was never invited to one of your husband's parties. Maybe it was her who dreamt up the idea of conning me into looking for Maxwell.'

She ignored the theorising. 'You mentioned other people who knew him. There were no other women, were there, Mr Lomax?'

I looked her straight in the eye. 'If there were I certainly didn't come across any, Mrs Bergman.'

She sighed her relief. Her mouth and chin were trembling and tears still flowed. She said, 'Take me to him now. For Heaven's sake take me to him.'

* ★ *

I made her finish the whisky, then took her down into the basement and led her into the laundry room.

'Why have you brought me here?'

I didn't answer. I had to get it over with. I let go of her arm, wrestled with the catch and threw back the lid of the big deep freeze. I pulled out the packages I'd crammed in a couple of days earlier and started on the layer beneath. I heard a ragged intake of breath close behind me, then saw the tallow coloured fingers. When I flung aside the next sack she let out the breath in a scream.

Blue eyes, opaque with cataracts of frost, stared blindly up at us. The gaping mouth, with its thick sensual lips, was distorted in a death rictus. Teeth, like fragments of dirty ice, protruded from gums blackened by congealed blood; blood which had overflowed and frozen in a dark ribbon across the grey cheek.

She fell on her knees, clutching the ice-cold rim of the freezer, oblivious to its cold. Her breathing was harsh, open-mouthed, laboured, disturbing the misty curtain of air that was escaping into the room. She slowly reached out a hand, placed it over the blue hole in his brow, began to caress the grey, frost hardened flesh with great tenderness.

'Tonee,' she keened, 'Tonee, Tonee, Tonee,' each time louder, until the word became a nerve-shattering scream.

20

I posted Maxwell's notebook to Barfield C.I.D., then followed developments in the press. Banner headlines began to spell out terse messages: gangland shoot-outs, slayings, drug hauls, freezer victims.

The body in the freezer didn't seem to give Mrs Bergman too many problems with the police. Maybe even hard boiled cops are suckers for a pretty face and the weak-little-woman routine. Or maybe she really had been nothing more than another plaything of Tony Maxwell's. She didn't mention me to the police. Perhaps she thought I knew more than I did. Whatever the reason, I was grateful. But then, she didn't pay me either. When I gently raised the matter after a discreet interval she equally gently explained how big mortgages and the correct clothes and all that tiresome business entertaining left the widows of company directors desperately short of ready cash. Nothing changes: the rich girl gets the pleasure, the poor guy gets the bailiffs.

I toyed with the idea of taking the fees out of the little nest egg Maxwell had been building up by ripping-off the no-hopers, but somehow I couldn't touch the dirty drug-money. I had to swallow my pride and phone round some of the big outfits that owed me. I managed to get enough in to keep afloat. I didn't get the waiting room chairs and the filing cabinets back. They'd already been auctioned-off for a fiver. So I rented some new gear; I figured the bailiffs may as well snatch a hire firm's stuff next time.

★　★　★

I waited six weeks for the dust to settle, then motored over to the high-rise council flats where the girl Maxwell had nicknamed Cleo lived. I tapped on the glass door. Summer had gone and a cold wind was stirring the litter on the access deck. The day was dying fast. I peered over the balustrade. Down in the canyon between the concrete towers it was almost dark.

'Yes?'

I turned. She was standing in the doorway, the light behind her.

'Hullo, Miss Soames.'

She looked at me, a puzzled frown creasing her smooth dark skin.

'Lomax,' I reminded, 'Paul Lomax.'

Recognition dawned. 'Oh, sure. The private investigator.' Her smile was wide and friendly.

'May I come in and have a word with you?'

She didn't say anything, just stepped aside and waved me in. I walked ahead of her, through the kitchen and into the unlit sitting room. She nodded towards one of the chairs with fluorescent-green fur cushions. I sat down, she curled up on the eye-sore facing mine.

'How are you?' I asked.

'Okay,' she said, and gave me a brave little grin. Black hair, cut in the Cleopatra style, was lustrous, almond eyes bright, skin clear. The now visible pregnancy seemed to be suiting her.

'Tony's dead, isn't he?'

I nodded.

'Somebody told me they'd seen it in the papers. Did you ever get to talk to him?'

'No,' I said. 'But I came across this.' I pulled out the manilla envelopes and handed them to her. 'Six thousand pounds. He left it in a safe deposit box with a note saying it had to be given to you.'

I figured just for once the victim ought to get the spoils.

She gazed down at the envelopes, bewildered by the sudden windfall.

'I'm glad I'm having his kid,' she said softly. 'And now he's dead the kid's all mine. I've never had anything that was all mine before, something no one can take away from me.'

I pushed myself out of the chair and half turned towards the door. Through the high window of that mean council flat I could see the first evening stars pricking the cold darkness beyond the town and the moors, mingling with the lights that gleamed in the huge villas perched on the crest of Mount St Joseph.

'Don't tell anyone you've got that kind of money,' I warned. 'Get it in the bank tomorrow and don't say where it came from.'

'Thanks,' she said. 'I won't talk. Was there anything else in the note?'

'Note?'

'The one Tony left with the money.'

'Oh, no,' I said. 'Just a few words scribbled on a piece of paper saying the money was for you.'

There's a limit to how many lies even I can tell.

THE END

We do hope that you have enjoyed reading this large print book.

Did you know that all of our titles are available for purchase?

We publish a wide range of high quality large print books including:
Romances, Mysteries, Classics
General Fiction
Non Fiction and Westerns

Special interest titles available in large print are:
The Little Oxford Dictionary
Music Book, Song Book
Hymn Book, Service Book

Also available from us courtesy of Oxford University Press:
Young Readers' Dictionary
(large print edition)
Young Readers' Thesaurus
(large print edition)

For further information or a free brochure, please contact us at:
Ulverscroft Large Print Books Ltd.,
The Green, Bradgate Road, Anstey,
Leicester, LE7 7FU, England.
Tel: (00 44) **0116 236 4325**
Fax: (00 44) **0116 234 0205**

Jimmy Ellis believes his parents have died in a car crash when as a young boy he is taken to live with relatives in Australia. The years pass happily, then the nightmare comes. Terrifying images flit through his mind in the dark — all through the eyes of a child, a witness to grisly events seventeen years before. He begins to delve into the past, and soon he finds himself on the trail of a double murderer — a murderer who is prepared to kill again.

THE DEAD TALE-TELLERS

John Newton Chance

Jonathan Blake always kept appointments. He had kept many, in all sorts of places, at all sorts of times, but never one like that one he kept in the house in the woods in the fading light of an October day. It seemed a perfect, peaceful place to visit and perhaps take tea and muffins round the fire. But at this appointment his footsteps dragged, for he knew that inside the house the men with whom he had that date were already dead . . .

DEATH IN RETREAT

George Douglas

On a day of retreat for clergy at
Overdale House, a resident guest,
Martin Pender, is foully murdered.
The primary task of the Regional
Homicide Squad is to track down the
bogus parson who joined the retreat.
Subsequent events show that serious
political motives lie behind the killing,
but the basic lead to it all is missing.
Then, three young tearaways corner
the killer in the woods, and a chess
problem, set out on a board, yields
vital evidence.

THE DEAD DON'T SCREAM

Leonard Gribble

Why had a woman screamed in Knightsbridge? Anthony Slade, the Yard's popular Commander of X2, sets out to investigate. Furthering the same end is Ken Surridge, a PR executive from a Northern consortium. Like Slade, Surridge wants to know why financier Shadwell Staines was shot and why a very scared girl appeared wearing a woollen housecoat. Before any facts can be discovered the girl takes off and Surridge gives chase, with Slade hot on his heels . . .